A Mexican Boy in Early Texas

For my dear grandchildren Mikayla + Addy

POLI

with love

A Mexican Boy in Early Texas

a novel by

Jay Neugeboren

[signature] gp
12/14

Illustrations by Tom Leamon

25th Anniversary Edition

Texas Tech University Press

The paper used in this book meets the minimum requirements of
ANSI/NISO Z39.48-1992 (R1997). ∞

Cover Design by Ashley Beck

Library of Congress Control Number: 2014951042
ISBN (paper): 978-0-89672-905-6

14 15 16 17 18 19 20 21 22 / 9 8 7 6 5 4 3 2 1

Texas Tech University Press
Box 41037 | Lubbock, Texas 79409-1037 USA
800.832.4042 | ttup@ttu.edu | www.ttupress.org

Dedicated to my sons, Aaron and Eli.

Author's Note

When *Poli: A Mexican Boy in Early Texas* was first published in 1989, the Hispanic population of Texas numbered some four and a half million people and represented thirty-two percent of the state's population. Now, a quarter of a century later, the Hispanic population numbers more than ten million and represents nearly forty percent of the state's population. It is my hope that Poli will inform—and inspire—young Hispanic men and women, while also educating other young Texans, along with readers everywhere, about the role this remarkable Mexican-American, José Policarpo Rodriguez, played in the exciting, formative years of Texas history.

I am grateful to Texas Tech University Press for re-issuing this book on the twenty-fifth anniversary of its original publication.

Jay Neugeboren
New York City
July 28, 2014

Preface

José Policarpo Rodriguez was born in Zaragosa, Mexico, on January 26, 1829, at a time when Texas was part of the Republic of Mexico, and the Rio Grande ran peacefully through the northern province of Coahuila. This book is based upon Poli's memoirs, passed on to me by Gladys Spann Matthews, who taught two of Poli's grandchildren in the public schools of Austin, Texas.

One day when she asked her class to write about their families, she received a composition from one of his grandsons entitled "José Policarpo Rodriguez—the Most Famous Guide in Texas History." Gladys Matthews told the family she thought Poli's biography should be written, and they offered her the use of his memoirs, which he dictated to the Reverend D. W. Carter, D.D., at various times from 1892 to 1897. The memoir was published in 1897 by the Publishing House of the Methodist Episcopal Church, South, under the title *The Old Guide*.

Years later, when Gladys Matthews and I were teaching together at the Saddle River Country Day School in Saddle River, New Jersey, she plunked a fat brown envelope down on the table next to me at lunch one afternoon and declared, "Well, I once tried to make a book out of all this and I couldn't do it. You're a writer, so now it's your turn."

Gladys Matthews was then in her mid-eighties and she was at least as blunt and generous as she had ever been. Along with drafts of the book she had attempted to write, she gave me a typed copy of Poli's memoirs, her research notes, transcriptions of anecdotes she heard from Poli's children and grandchildren, and a suggestion—one which came in the form of a loving admonition: that I use the material as the basis for a fictionalized biography. *Poli* is, then, a work of fiction, based upon the major facts and events of Poli's life.

"It takes a keen, smart man to trail," goes a Texas saying. "Not many can do it." Poli could do it. By all accounts he could do it as well as any guide who ever trailed the rivers, plains, hills, and forests of Texas. But he was more than just an excellent and famous guide. At various times in his long life, he was also, among other things, a surveyor, a scout, a hunter, a Texas Ranger, an Indian fighter, a ranchman, a Keeper of Camels, and a preacher.

Although I have taken some imaginative liberties— inventing dialogue and characters here and there, shifting and/or combining some elements for dramatic or narrative ends—the story I tell is, in its essentials, true to the facts of Poli's life: He came north from Zaragosa to San Antonio with his father when he was a boy; he grew up with Comanches; he surveyed territory for the Republic of Texas and the U. S. Army; he fought against warring Indians; he mapped settlements for the nineteenth-century German settlers in Texas; he was the first non-Indian to discover the Big Bend Country and Cascade Caverns; and he refused to fight in either the Mexican-American War or the Civil War, though during these conflicts he joined with and was Captain of the San Antonio Home Guard.

I have diverged from and embellished upon some particulars of his story in order to render more fully a sense of what life was like for Mexicans and Texans, and especially for Mexican-Texans who grew up and came of age with the State of Texas during its formative years, from 1839 to 1846. This, rather than literal fidelity to the actuality of Poli's life, is what I have aimed for in telling the tale of a Mexican boy in nineteenth-century Texas.

Jay Neugeboren

Contents

Poli

A Mexican Boy in Early Texas

Chapter 1

POLI COMES TO TEXAS

The Mexican boy raced along the river's edge, then veered to his left, away from the calm blue of the Medina. The Indians were gaining on him. He darted past a large patch of yellow rabbit brush, the drumming of horses's hooves pounding inside his skull. He glanced behind, then streaked across the prairie. He saw specks of pale green mesquite where he and his father had made their camp the night before, and the green specks seemed to rise from the prairie, to spin in circles. He felt dizzy.

The cries of Indians roared towards him like ice cold night winds. He cut back sharply, toward the river. *"Indios!"* he cried. *"Indios!"*

A thin line of smoke rose lazily from the campfire. He saw his horse, Hermano, tied to a tree by the river bank. He raced on. The campfire seemed to expand, to explode—the flames entering Poli's eyes, setting the inside of his head ablaze.

"Indios!" he cried again. *"Indios bravos!"*

Poli knew that many Indian bands were friendly toward Mexicans—they traded with Mexicans and helped defend them from raids by Texans. Some had even fought with the Mexican Army against Sam Houston. But he also knew that there were Indians who were friendly toward no man—Mexican, Texan, or American. There were Indians who raided villages north and south of the Rio Grande for revenge, for goods, and for young boys who would serve them as slaves.

He ran on, tripped, stood, slipped again, stumbled, scraped his knees. Terrified, he rose quickly and—his small brown body erect, his muscles taut—he faced the oncoming warriors.

Slashes of red paint blazed across their chests. Poli gripped the handle of his bowie knife. Dust swirled in front of him so that for a moment, as they reined in their horses, the Indians disappeared. The dust fell away and Poli saw a strip of gold—a ribbon tied to the tail of a chestnut-colored horse. The Indian who rode the horse leapt to the ground and shouted. Bright feathers circled his shield. A second warrior, still on horseback, raised a long lance, its point aimed for Poli's heart. Poli drew his knife.

"Poli!"

Poli turned. His father stood behind him.

"Put away your knife."

Señor Rodriguez walked past Poli, his arm outstretched in a sign of peace. The Indian now held a white buffalo skin in his arms, and offered it to Poli's father. The Indian spoke a language Poli could not understand

and then, to Poli's surprise, the Indian stated his father's name: "José Antonio Rodriguez—"

Señor Rodriguez accepted the robe—a sign of friendship, Poli knew—and spoke in Spanish: "I am José Antonio Rodriguez, of Zaragosa, and this is José Policarpo Rodriguez, the son of my old age. We crossed the Rio Grande eight days ago. We come in peace."

"*Mañana*," the Indian said.

"*Mañana por la mañana*," Señor Rodriguez replied.

The Indian mounted his pony. He and his braves turned and rode across the prairie, their lances upright, the ribbons that hung from their horses' tails—red, blue, and gold—fluttering in the dust like small bright birds.

Poli's father walked toward the camp, the white robe in his arms. Poli sheathed his knife, hesitated, then followed.

"How did they know your name?"

"They're Comanches," Señor Rodriguez said. "From the tribe of the Penatekas—the Honey-Eaters."

"But how did they know your name, and why did you tell them mine?"

Poli's father set the white robe upon the ground, but said nothing.

"I saw their war paint," Poli said. "As soon as I sighted them from the river bank I came to warn you."

"Yes."

"You talked of *mañana*—what will happen then? Tell me. Please—"

"Go and build up the fire," Señor Rodriguez replied. "You'll need your food and your sleep, for tomorrow I'm sending you to live with the Comanches."

Chapter 2

¡VOLADOR!

Poli pressed his cheek to Hermano's muzzle. The pony, a brown and white roan Poli's brother Juan had given him for his tenth birthday, whinnied with pleasure. Poli stroked its head, touched its ear. The Comanches, he knew, split the left ears of their horses, to mark them.

When they had pitched camp three nights before, Poli's father promised they would stay by the Medina for a few days only—until he found work in San Antonio. Although San Antonio was now part of the Republic of Texas, most of its citizens were Mexicans, men like themselves who had come north in search of new lives. Texas was no longer the northernmost province of Mexico, but an independent republic, established three years before when Sam Houston had defeated General Santa Anna at the battle of San Jacinto.

Poli wanted their new life to be as wonderful as his father claimed it would be; yet left alone in their camp while his father spent the days looking for work in town, Poli found himself thinking of Zaragosa. He thought of his mother, who had died the year before of cholera, as had many in the village, including his sister-in-law Raquela and three of his cousins. He thought too of the friends he had left behind—of chasing wild turkeys and rabbits with them in the high grass near the corn fields, or smoking corn-sticks under live oaks by the river. He thought of his brothers and sisters, his cousins and aunts and uncles—of working side by side with them in fields full of ripe corn, squash, peppers, yams, and tomatoes.

Each day after his father left for San Antonio, Poli performed his chores—fishing, hunting, gathering firewood, fetching water, caring for Hermano—and while he did, he often imagined night coming on, his father not returning. He tried to think of what he would do were he left alone. Would he attempt to find his way home? Would he journey to San Antonio to search for his father? And if his father never came back . . .

When his father did return at the end of each day, Poli was as frightened of telling him his fears as he had been of being left alone. He thought, too, of how happy he and his family and friends had been in Zaragosa— during those times when there had been enough food, and when they had, after the fall harvest, rejoiced during the annual fiesta.

In Zaragosa, Poli's father had been greatly admired —a man who had fought for Mexico's independence, the only man in the village who dared, during the fiesta, to climb the *volador*.

Poli saw himself among friends, gazing at the platform seventy feet above the ground. He saw Señor Pasquale, who owned the hacienda, sitting on the balcony of his mansion with his family. Like the owners of all the haciendas in Mexico, Señor Pasquale was absolute ruler of his vast estate, judge and executioner in all disputes. He required of all the families on his hacienda that they work for him without pay each Monday, that they clear, sow, and gather twenty *mecates* of corn for him when they married and had families. Like his friends, Poli feared and hated Señor Pasquale. For the right to use his water, Señor Pasquale required that all the workers and farmers on his land be obliged, when the church bell struck five times, to leave their own fields and work for a meager one *real* a day, not even enough to buy a day's corn and water. And of the fruits of their labor—from their own small fields and from what food they could grow on the *ejidos*, the communal lands, he required that they give him half the produce.

Still, the time of the fiesta was joyous, and when Poli saw Señor Pasquale raise a white-gloved hand—the signal to begin—his heart was glad, for it was then that Poli's father, his arms winged with painted feathers, leapt from the platform.

Poli watched the ropes that held his father, saw his older brothers rotate the platform so that as the ropes unwound his father circled downwards in the air—rising and falling like a great soaring bird!

Just so, Señor Rodriguez explained to Poli, had the Aztecs performed the feat for centuries before them. When Poli stood among his friends afterwards and explained to them who the Aztecs were, the other boys moved closer to him, their eyes glowing. To have a father who dared to climb the *volador* and fly like the ancient gods . . . .

"Here, son." Poli turned. His father held the white buffalo robe toward him. "This robe is for you, to take with you tomorrow morning."

Poli spoke before he thought: "I didn't come to Texas to live like an Indian."

"These Indians are our friends," Señor Rodriguez said. "The paint on their faces wasn't war paint but their sign that they'll soon set out on a great buffalo hunt."

"I thought we came here so we could be Texans." Poli protested. "Not Mexicans."

Señor Rodriguez clutched the robe so tightly his knuckles turned white, like the buffalo skin. "We will always be Mexicans," he said.

"Then why did we leave?"

Señor Rodriguez looked beyond Poli. His fists opened and the rage in his eyes washed away, so that they were calm and clear, the color of smooth earth at the bottom of a clear stream. "This was once Mexico too," he said.

"I'm sorry for what I said before," Poli said. "But sometimes when you're gone all day, I worry that you

won't return—that I'll have to go back to Zaragosa by
myself."

"That's why the Comanches came to us."

"I don't understand. I thought we came here to
find work and a home in San Antonio. Why then are
you sending me to live with Comanches?"

"Because they promised you to me."

"Promised me?"

"As a gift for my old age."

"I don't understand."

"Come," Señor Rodriguez said. "Come sit by the
fire with me and I'll tell you the story. It's time."

Poli sat across from his father. In the west the sun
was setting and long lines of red and orange trailed along
the horizon like ribbons of fire.

"When I was a young man," Señor Rodriguez
began, "and your mother and I lived on Señor Pasquale's
land, and in the years before you were born, I had five
sons and two daughters."

Poli counted: Juan, Roberto, Miguel, Sanchez,
Elena, Teresa . . . Who was the fifth son?

"Before you, there was another Policarpo—Rafael
Policarpo Rodriguez—my first-born child, whom I loved
dearly. I taught him to hunt and to ride and to care
for Señor Pasquale's horses. I held him when he cried,
I scolded him when he was mischievous, and I watched
him grow even as I've watched you grow.

"Then, in 1821, when our people fought against

Spain for independence, we left Zaragosa to join in the war. Rafael was fourteen years old. We joined with the guerilla leader Guerrero and battled against the armies who rode under the Spanish General O'Donoju. Ten months later, when the Spaniards surrendered and Mexico became, we thought, a free state, I returned to Zaragosa."

"Alone?"

"Yes. In the years that followed I often wondered why I'd fought at all. For we seemed only to have replaced one tyrant with another, and this time the tyrant was of our own blood. General Iturbide ruled as the Spanish viceroy had—with great cruelty. When he was banished, Guerrero and Santa Anna established a republic and once again, as ever, our hearts filled with hope, and once again the hope was butchered. We've had many governments since—many leaders who've told us of all the freedoms we've gained—yet in Zaragosa, little ever changed. We continued to live as we lived before, subject to the will and power of the large landowners."

Señor Rodriguez stirred the fire. Poli watched the glowing coals and recalled the rage he had often seen in his father's eyes when he would go with him to the company store from which all those who lived on the hacienda were compelled to buy their food, clothing, and supplies. No matter how hard they worked, or how bountiful the produce, their debt to Señor Pasquale never seemed to diminish.

The parable of the loaves is at work, Señor

Rodriguez would tell his family, with bitterness. Each time I pay some of my debt, more debt appears to replace it.

"When I returned from the war, I returned alone. Your brother Rafael was dead. I vowed to have no more children," Señor Rodriguez continued, "and I didn't permit Rafael's name to be spoken in my presence. Life went on, of course. Your brothers and sisters grew and married and received their *suertes*—their individual plots of land on the hacienda, from which they tried to scratch lives for themselves. My guns, I thought, were put away forever.

"Then, in the eighth year after I returned from Mexico City, word reached us that a band of Comanches was approaching. In those days, as now, the Comanche hunting grounds extended for hundreds of miles, all across the great plains, from Kansas to Oklahoma and Texas and Coahuila. The Comanches were famed as the finest of horsemen, and feared because when they made war, they took captives.

"There are warriors who ride today with Comanche bands, feathers in their hair and war paint across their cheeks—warriors who, like yourself and your brothers, were once small boys in Mexican villages such as Zaragosa.

"In my own lifetime they'd never roamed as far south as our village, but their tribes, we learned, had been depleted by smallpox the previous year—the disease brought by the white man moving west onto their hunting grounds—and to replenish their numbers they'd become more warlike and far-roaming.

"I met with the men of Zaragosa and we prepared our defenses. We posted scouts daily on the northern and western trails that led from town. All was quiet for several weeks. Then, at the end of the summer, the Comanches appeared suddenly one afternoon when Zaragosa, in the time of its siesta, was quiet. They rode into the marketplace and the villagers fled.

"The Comanches didn't pursue. Instead, they dismounted and began to eat. Their raiding party had no more than two dozen members, and the villagers who escaped soon reached our house, the first one inside the grounds of the hacienda. I sent Juan to town. He made his way there by foot, climbed to the church tower and rang the bells. Within minutes more than fifty of us had gathered by the little falls of the Sarajito River.

"We sent two scouts ahead—your brother Miguel, and a boy named Cruz. Only Miguel returned. The Indians, he reported, remained in the market place, loading their horses with supplies. Cruz was captured.

"We decided to converge on the market place from both north and south, thereby cutting off any escape route. To the west were Señor Pasquale's storehouses, where the old men of Zaragosa could lie in wait, shooting from windows and roofs—and to the east, as you know, was the gorge.

"The battle was brief and gruesome. The Comanches were outnumbered and in the close quarters of the market place they were unable to make use of their superior horsemanship. When they took flight along the northern trail, we entered the market place to tend to the wounded and gather the dead. To our surprise, the Comanches returned. There were only eight of them left, but they fought more bravely to recover the bodies of their dead tribesmen than they'd fought for their own lives.

"It was then that I did something I hadn't known I was going to do.

"I walked into the center of the village square, a white handkerchief tied to my rifle. I shouted to the Comanches that I came in peace. And all the while, in my mind, I was seeing your brother Rafael's face, as if he were there with me. I saw him as he'd been eight years before, when he lay dead on a field outside Mexico City. I saw him being lowered into a soldier's grave and while this memory was in my head, I called to the Comanches to put away their weapons.

"The Comanches turned their horses in furious circles but they didn't attack. I told them they should take their dead away and never visit our village again.

"There were some who thought I was mad, yet while the Comanches worked to rescue their dead, none among us moved. When they were done, and had set Cruz free, and when the dead bodies of their warriors lay across their horses, the leader of their band rode to me and spoke, in Spanish. He told me that there would be a place for me in the Indian spirit world. Then he cried mightily and declared that, being a man of visions and a great chief of his people, he could prophesy the future.

"He was Ten Bears—Parra-Wa-Samen—and his name was known as far as buffalo roamed. He twirled his lance in the air five times, and spun his horse around twice. Because I allowed him to retrieve his sons, he proclaimed, I myself, before twelve moons passed, would be blessed with a son who would comfort me even into my years of darkness.

"Then he turned and rode off."

Señor Rodriguez stopped. He had not been looking at Poli while he talked, but now he did. In the cool night air, the sound of live oak sticks crackled like heat lightning. "The braves who came today and asked me my name, and for the year in which you were born, are from Chief Ten Bears' tribe. You'll go and live with them for a week, as their guest, until it's time for them to depart for their great hunt."

Chapter 3

EAGLE BLOOD

When Poli awoke the next morning, he saw that Hermano was already saddled, the white buffalo robe spread across its haunches. A young Indian boy stood above Poli, blocking the sun that rose in the east. Poli drew his bowie knife from its place under his bedroll.

"I'm Eagle Blood. I've come to take you with me to our camp."

Poli stood and faced the Indian. Eagle Blood was slightly taller than Poli, his skin gleaming like burnished copper in the dim morning light. His eyes were outlined in black and his lashes were plucked; his chest was bare, his black hair parted in the middle, a single braid falling to each side of his face. He wore no shoes.

"I'm glad you speak Spanish," Poli said, "since I only know a few words of Comanche."

"I'll teach you," Eagle Blood said. "But we must leave now. It's late."

Poli pulled on his boots.

"My father told me that your tribe, the Honey-Eaters, once were enslaved to the Catholic missions, where you helped them to build and to farm. You learned Spanish there."

Eagle Blood turned away. "Others call us Honey-Eaters, to make us into women. We call ourselves Numunahs, which means The People."

Poli's father stood by the campfire, frying corn dough in pork fat—the *masa* Poli loved. Gesturing to Eagle Blood to follow, Poli walked toward the campfire. Poli's father handed him a plate, and Poli offered his food to Eagle Blood.

"The day grows shorter," Eagle Blood said.

Poli ate quickly, then approached Hermano. He reached under Hermano's belly and unhitched the saddle.

"All Mexicans ride with saddles," Eagle Blood stated.

Poli said nothing. He removed Hermano's saddle, placed it on the ground, then took his lariat from the saddle and made a noose. He slipped the noose around Hermano's head and twisted the lariat around the lower jaw to complete the hackamore, the halter by which he would guide his pony.

Then he leapt on. He did everything the way his father taught him—the night before!—and to his surprise he found himself sitting upright on Hermano's warm back, a piece of rope clutched in his right hand.

"My father said that Comanche is the word the

Ute Indians gave you. It means enemy."

Eagle Blood mounted his tan and white pinto. "We'll talk later," he said. "Mexican boys talk so much they think their words will make the sun stop."

Señor Rodriguez came to Poli. "You learn quickly, my son," he said, smiling. "Things will go well for you in Eagle Blood's camp. I'm sure of it."

"*Adios*, Papa," Poli said. "I'll miss you. I hope you find work soon."

"*Vaya con Dios.*" Señor Rodriguez stepped back, waved. "I'll see you in a week."

"Let's go!" Poli said to Eagle Blood, and as he did he turned Hermano abruptly—too abruptly, for he almost slipped off—and headed south. He glanced sideways, to see if Eagle Blood noticed. Eagle Blood stared straight ahead. Poli clenched the lariat tightly in his hand. He hoped Eagle Blood would think he had been riding bareback for a long time.

Then the two boys streaked across the prairie, side by side, the warm morning wind in their faces. A friend! Poli told himself. A friend of my own!

When they neared the spot by the Medina River where the Comanches were now settled, six miles southwest of Poli's camp, Eagle Blood slowed down. Poli stayed a few paces behind, and, to ease his nervousness, he imagined that he was watching an old Mexican *campesino* riding to market on a burro. When Poli laughed, Eagle Blood glared at him.

"Boys laugh at air," he said. "Men do not."

Poli imagined Eagle Blood wearing a sombrero and a serape. He imagined Eagle Blood's pinto growing long ears.

"Why do you smile?" Eagle Blood asked.

"Boys give away secrets," Poli replied. "Men do not."

Eagle Blood dismounted and told Poli to wait for him. Soon the Comanches would journey north toward the Texas panhandle to hunt the great herds of buffalo, and, as Señor Rodriguez had explained, they would prepare for the hunt with a week of feasting and games.

The Comanche tepees were lined up along the river in rows—not, as Poli expected, in circles—and they stretched for at least a mile. The tepees were thirteen or fourteen feet high, covered with buffalo hides and pinned, at the entrances, with pieces of wood. They faced east, toward the rising sun, and many of them were decorated with paintings of horses, birds, buffalo, and warriors. In the bright morning light, they looked like small jeweled pyramids.

Between the tepees Poli saw racks: Y-shaped pieces of wood about five feet high that were stuck into the ground some ten feet apart, poles resting in the notches, animal skins hanging across the poles. As Poli watched the Indians work, he wondered if some of them had once been Mexicans. He wondered if he would see any of the famous black Indians—the Negro slaves Comanches sometimes captured from Americans.

In the camp, women were preparing food and making arrows, young braves were pursuing one another with pointed sticks, dogs were roaming among the

tepees, girls were pinning buffalo hides to the ground
and scraping them with pieces of bone—and suddenly,
watching it all, Poli had little desire to tease Eagle Blood,
little desire to laugh. Suddenly Poli found himself long-
ing for Zaragosa.

Despite all the misery he and his father had
experienced there, it was still the only home he had
ever known. Poli wished he could be sitting at the table
with his brothers and sisters and their families, eating
a dinner of *tamales* and *frijoles*. He wished he could be
carrying gourds and corn to the silos in which the
produce was stored, or hunting along the banks of the
Sarajito with his friends, or watching wild pigs rooting
for acorns among the scrub oak.

Poli turned toward the north: Hundreds of horses
grazed there, and Poli envied them their ease. He wished
he could be sitting outside his adobe home in Zaragosa,
talking with his friends of all he was discovering about
Texas and San Antonio and Comanches . . .

Poli looked toward the camp again. Eagle Blood
approached, a group of about fifteen braves with him.
Poli smiled—he wanted to please them—but when the
group reached him, they said nothing and formed a
silent circle around him.

Poli dismounted. The braves moved closer. They
touched Poli, examined his breeches and buckskin shirt,
felt the hard toes of his leather boots. Some of them
spoke to him in Comanche dialect and offered him their
bows and arrows, for inspection. Their cheeks were
daubed with red paint, their hair parted and braided,

and like Eagle Blood, they had plucked their lashes so that their eyes seemed to glisten—to pierce his own like the eyes of owls.

"My brothers are your brothers," Eagle Blood said. "We all know what your father did when we were in Mexico, and so they say to you that you are their friend for as long as water runs and the grass grows."

Poli spread his arms, showing his open palms. "And I'm your friend for as long as rivers run down to the sea," he said.

A young brave came forward and, his words carefully rehearsed, spoke in Spanish: "We call this the land of the *Tejas*—from our word for friend. You're with us in the land of the *Tejas*, Poli."

"Yes," Poli said. His heart thumped wildly against his chest, as if it wanted to fly!

Eagle Blood handed Poli a bow and a fistful of arrows.

"I've never used a bow before," Poli said.

"We'll teach you."

Poli followed Eagle Blood and the others into the woods that lay south of the camp. They moved quietly along the forest floor until they came to a clearing. Eagle Blood explained that because Comanches usually fought and hunted from horses, they used the short bow, which was about three feet long and made of osage orange. The arrows were of dogwood, cut so that from feather to point they were equal to the distance from elbow to fingertip. The string was fashioned from buffalo sinew, and Eagle Blood showed Poli how to draw it to his chin and sight the target along the shaft of the arrow. The crucial thing, Eagle Blood said, was to keep both the hand that held the bow and the hand that held the arrow perfectly steady, even after the arrow had been released.

At the end of the afternoon, when Poli was salting a rabbit to take back to his father, the young braves stood around and watched. Poli had killed two rabbits on his first day, and he hoped his new friends were proud of how quickly he learned.

Poli and the young Comanche braves prepared their own fire and food—rabbit cooked with squash, tomato, and mustard seed; they ate apart from the elders of the tribe, and after the meal they fed and watered their horses, banked the fires, readied their bows, arrows, and knives for the coming day, scraped and cleaned the skins and set them on racks to dry. Then the braves returned to their families, to sleep.

Eagle Blood prepared a place outside his own tepee for Poli. Poli thanked him, but when the noise of the camp subsided, he found himself still awake, his ears alert to the slightest night sound, his mind alive with pictures—of raiding parties riding into Mexico, of soldiers dying in battle, of Indians burning, of white men being scalped. He saw himself wandering across an immense desert and felt his tongue swelling so that it filled his mouth and he could not breathe. He wondered where his father was. He wondered if his brothers and sisters were thinking of him. In the darkness, he drew his knife from its sheath, let his cheek lie against its cool steel.

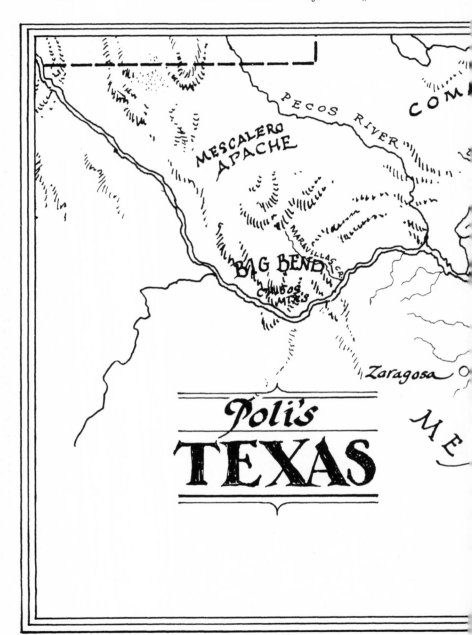

Chapter 4

WAR GAMES

The blade quivered in the hard ground less than a foot from Poli's head.

"Mexicans sleep like dead men," Eagle Blood declared.

Poli pulled the knife from the ground and saw that it was his own. He sheathed it. "How did you do that?" he asked.

"It's time for our war games," Eagle Blood said. "Come on. The others have already eaten, but I brought you something to drink."

Eagle Blood handed Poli a deerskin water bag. Poli drank, then followed Eagle Blood toward the spot where the braves were waiting, on the flat prairie north of the camp. The boys spoke to Poli, some of them using Spanish words. For the first time since he had met Eagle Blood, Poli found no words. He felt embarrassed, he realized, for he did not know their ways of doing things and he was afraid they might think him weak and foolish.

Eagle Blood mounted his pinto from the right side, took a shield from one of the braves. The shield was about three feet long, an oval decorated with paintings of buffalo and deer, and trimmed with feathers, dyed porcupine quills, and bear claws. Eagle Blood rode off, then stopped and turned. He was several hundred feet away when the other braves took up their bows and arrows and set themselves in two lines, facing one another. Eagle Blood shouted and the braves drew back the strings of their bows. Eagle Blood streaked towards them, his body pressed against his pony's neck.

When Eagle Blood reached the lines of young warriors, Poli gasped; for as Eagle Blood passed through, his shield moving from side to side, the warriors drew their strings and launched their arrows at him. Poli touched the handle of his knife and moved forward; when he saw the arrows bounce from Eagle Blood's shield, he stopped.

And when, a few minutes later, Eagle Blood stood next to Poli, Poli saw only a few small bruises on his thighs and arms. Eagle Blood gave one of the arrows to Poli. Poli held it by the shaft: The deadly arrowhead, he saw, was wrapped in a piece of antelope skin, the skin stuffed with bits of leather and tied with a strip of rawhide.

Poli watched as other braves played the game. The next boy, Horse Back, was not as skillful as Eagle Blood; when he completed his run, his face and chest were covered with large red welts.

Eagle Blood explained that the shield was made

from a single buffalo hide, taken from the neck of a bull, the hide toughened by being soaked in a brine solution and then stretched over a dogwood frame. Each brave painted his own shield, and placed the sign of the tribe in its central circle.

"We decorate the shields with bears' teeth to show that we're hunters, with the tails of horses to show that we're raiders . . . and with scalps to show that we're warriors." Eagle Blood set his shield carefully on the ground, next to his bow and arrows. "The shield is sacred and may not be given to another to use. For our next game, I'll let you use my horse. But first, watch. There goes Black Moon."

Poli saw a white pony galloping at full speed, braves shooting their arrows at the horse.

"All I see is a horse," Poli said. "Is Black Moon a white horse?"

"Look!"

Again Eagle Blood pointed and now Poli saw an Indian sitting on the horse. Poli blinked. Eagle Blood laughed.

"This game's called The Loop." Eagle Blood led Poli to his own horse and showed him the loop—a braid made of rawhide, which he dropped beneath the horse's chest, then brought around the horse's neck, from both sides, and braided into the mane.

Another horse raced by. As the braves shot their arrows, the rider dropped to the far side of the horse, his elbow and upper arm falling into the loop as if it were a sling. At the same time, he let his heel hang over the ridge of the horse's backbone. When he passed beyond the lines of young warriors, he sprang upright on his horse, using his heel for leverage.

"Now it's my turn," Eagle Blood said.

Eagle Blood rode off, turned, and raced toward the waiting braves. Poli watched him drop onto the far side of the pony; then, as the braves launched their arrows at him, Eagle Blood dropped away and, from the underside of the horse—while moving at full speed—shot arrows back at them.

When Eagle Blood returned, he told Poli he would now teach him how to play The Loop. He cautioned Poli about not riding too swiftly. Poli felt his heart beat wildly, however, and heard a ringing sound in his ears, as if they were covered with large sea shells. He dug in his heels and galloped across the prairie, determined to show his new friends he could do anything they could.

He circled back, shouted, then sped toward the waiting braves. When he was twenty yards away he let his body drop to the side of Eagle Blood's pony—the loop held his shoulder, his heel started to catch—and then he felt the shock of ground as he bumped down. Tucking his feet to his chest, he rolled away to avoid the pony's hooves.

The young braves neither mocked Poli nor encouraged him. Eagle Blood led Poli away from the others and instructed him again, patiently showing him exactly where to place his heel, how to coordinate the movements of arms, body, and legs. He helped Poli to make the loop and to braid it into Hermano's mane. Then he took a second strip of rawhide and fashioned it into a stirrup which could hold Poli's foot when Poli let his arm and shoulder drop down. He had Poli practice from a standing position first, and then while Hermano was trotting. Gradually he made Poli quicken the pace. For the rest of the afternoon—first with the extra stirrup, and then without—Poli practiced.

Only when he left the prairie with the other boys and was walking toward camp did he remember that he had not eaten all day long. He thought of the *charqui*—the dried meat, or "jerky," that he and his father carried with them in their saddle bags. He thought of wild boar basted with chili sauce, of tortillas filled with corn and beans, of the brown-fleshed *chictzapotl*—his favorite fruit—dripping its juices, glistening with jet-black seeds. When Eagle Blood spoke, it was as if his voice were coming from far away, from a dream some other Mexican boy was dreaming. "My father has asked you to eat with us tonight," Eagle Blood said.

Chapter 5

CHIEF TOSH-A-WAH

The skin beneath Poli's shoulder was raw—the loop had cut into it severely—but as he walked with Eagle Blood and the other braves, he vowed not to let them know of his pain.

They passed women braiding horsehair and making lassos, young girls attaching feathers to arrows. His mouth dry, Poli longed for some *atole*—a drink he and his friends in Zaragosa loved to make: fried corn dough mixed with water, sweetened with sugar and flavored with bits of chocolate and cinnamon. He wanted to tell Eagle Blood all about Zaragosa—about his friends and his family. He wanted to tell him how strange it felt: to feel such affection for a place he and his father had been glad to leave. But it was, he heard himself saying, as if in answer to an unasked question, the only childhood I had. It was my life. Can you understand?

Eagle Blood showed Poli the tepee where the old men of the tribe spent their days, smoking and retelling

tales of their younger life. "I call many of them father,"
Eagle Blood said, "because they're my father's brothers.
Their sons and daughters are my brothers and sisters."

Eagle Blood pushed aside the bearskin which hung
over the entrance to a tall tepee.

"This is my father, Tosh-a-wah—a great warrior
when he was young, a great peacemaker now that he
has years. His name is known wherever buffalo roam,
and feared wherever evil men gather to take our land
from us."

Chief Tosh-a-wah, a broad-chested man with a flat
wide nose, rose from his place beside the fire and placed
a large hand upon each of Poli's shoulders. A single
eagle feather was stuck into Chief Tosh-a-wah's scalplock,
a thunderbird painted on his chest. The tips of the first
two fingers on his left hand were missing.

Chief Tosh-a-wah lifted his head upwards and
prayed for Poli's safe passage into the spirit world.

Then, before Poli could react, the chief drew Poli's
knife from its sheath. The chief held the knife with both
hands, touched its blade to his chest. Eagle Blood translated his father's words.

"He tells you that Tosh-a-wah means Silver Knife,"
Eagle Blood said.

Chief Tosh-a-wah returned Poli's knife and gestured
to a buffalo skin that lay on the ground beside him.
Poli sat.

"I was in Zaragosa with Ten Bears," Chief Tosh-a-
wah began, "and like Ten Bears I too lost a son—a brother
to your brother Eagle Blood. I brought that son home

with me and cut my hair and gashed my body in mourn-
ing. On my son's grave I spilled the blood of his horse."
Chief Tosh-a-wah made a sweeping gesture with his
left hand, as if slaughtering the horse. "The Comanche
is not weak and blind like the pup of a dog when several
sleeps old. He is strong and far-sighted, like a grown
horse. My son died in Mexico and now you are in the
world, as it was foretold, the gift that would come to
your father in his years, a companion to him after his
wife was gone."

A young girl entered the tent.

"This is my sister, Tana-kawi," Eagle Blood said.
"Like yours, our mother too is gone into the spirit
world."

Tana-kawi put wood on the fire. With a long pole,
she opened and closed a flap at the top of the tepee,
creating a draft which drew the smoke out into the night
air. Then, in the campfire's pit, she began cooking. Poli
thought of his mother, grinding corn, then setting it
on the hot earthen griddle where she made him the
tortillas he loved. Poli felt as if he were in two places
at the same time.

Tana-kawi worked carefully, coating strips of buffalo
steak with a paste made from crushed blackberries. Eagle
Blood explained that if a Comanche warrior died in battle, one of his brothers would marry the dead warrior's
wife. That was why, from the time he could speak, he
had called all his uncles father and all his cousins
brother. For a people who were constantly at war, and
who lost many brave young men, it was one way of

maintaining the ongoing life of the tribe and the strength of family bonds.

Poli saw his mother again, saw a dark blue shawl being drawn across her face as she lay on her thin bed. He saw his three young cousins, buried at the same time his mother was buried. Poli thought of his brother Miguel's wife, dead before her daughter's first cry escaped into the world. Zaragosa! He imagined the landscape he loved stripped of all color and vegetation. Vultures circled downwards, tried to suck water from the hard ground, from black stones. Poli heard his father's voice: If Señor Pasquale cared as much for our lives as for his horses, this would not be.

Tana-kawi set wooden bowls before them, then sat down on the other side of Eagle Blood.

Chief Tosh-a-wah spoke: "Soon we'll go on our hunt and drive the Texans from our hunting grounds. It's good for you that you're a Mexican. We'll help return your land to you."

Chief Tosh-a-wah rose and spoke angrily: "If the Texans had kept out of my country there might have been peace. We have never gone to war—war has come to us.

"The Texans have brought sorrow into our tents and we went out from them as the buffalo bulls do when the cows are attacked. They've given guns to other Indians and instead of hunting the game set upon the earth for us all, these Indians have killed our braves, so that the warriors of my tribe cut short their hair for the dead."

Chief Tosh-a-wah sat. Tana-kawi placed a strip of meat in his bowl.

"If the Texans had kept out of my country," Chief Tosh-a-wah repeated, "there might have been peace. I was born upon the prairie where the wind blew free and there was nothing to break the light of the sun, and I will die there. Oh do not ask us to give up the buffalo for the sheep! Do not ask us to give up the buffalo for the sheep!"

Chief Tosh-a-wah cut a piece of meat from his steak and placed it in Poli's mouth.

"You are your father's son," he said.

When the meal was over, Tana-kawi offered a prayer of thanks—to the Sun, which was the Father of all things, and to the Earth, which was the Mother. Although she was only twelve, a year older than Eagle Blood, she had all the rights and responsibilities of an adult Comanche woman. Tana-kawi had built the tepee in which Poli now sat.

Tana-kawi turned to Poli: "Why did you come to the land of the *Tejas?*" she asked. "Why did you leave Mexico?"

Before Poli could reply, she rose and departed. Poli turned to Eagle Blood. He wanted to explain what his father had explained: that the land had been dry and unforgiving, that there was no longer enough food for his brothers and sisters and their children to eat. Even the prickly cactus had given up its store of nourishment and turned the color of dry limestone. He wanted to tell

Chief Tosh-a-wah about Señor Pasquale and how Mexicans lived on his hacienda as if they were still slaves to
the Spaniards. He wanted to tell them what life was like
on the haciendas of Mexico, where a few men owned
all—where Poli had seen Señor Pasquale's overseers
whip men, women, and children with switches until
they fainted, and where, when these families turned to
the church for consolation, the priests—who owned
more land than men like Señor Pasquale—counselled
submission, obedience, and hope for salvation in the
life to come.

But Poli and his father and their family and friends
still lived in *this* world. Poli wanted to tell Eagle Blood
that in this world he too, like the Comanches, wished
to be free—to go where he pleased, to hunt for his food,
to grow his own vegetables and fruit, to make his clothing and build his shelter and own his own land. If only
one could have one's own land, one could be free . . .

Poli knew, however, that the Comanches did not
believe one could buy or sell the earth upon which
humans walked and lived. They did not believe the land
could be divided or owned. The earth was created for
everybody and could never, therefore, be the property
of one man or of one people.

"My daughter knows that her questions are
answered not by words, but by time," Chief Tosh-a-wah
said. "And so she has given you her question. She is
your sister too."

"Why did you come to the land of the *Tejas*?" Eagle

Blood asked, as if he were intoning the words to a prayer.

"Why did you leave Mexico?" Chief Tosh-a-wah asked, as if answering his son.

Chapter 6

DEAD COMANCHES

Their faces daubed with red paint, the elders of the tribe gathered north of the camp. Poli stood next to Chief Tosh-a-wah and they watched an Indian boy set out a trail of arrows in two rows.

Chief Tosh-a-wah signalled: Eagle Blood streaked forward on his horse, dropped into his loop, snatched an arrow from the ground, and then—without slackening his speed—sprang back onto the horse's back, dropped to the other side, picked up the next arrow.

A half-minute later he raised a fistful of arrows into the air. The elders of the tribe shouted their praise.

Another boy sped forward, dropped into his loop, let his feet touch the ground, ran for several steps, then bounced back upon his horse. A third horse galloped across the prairie, a young Comanche behind it, clutching to its tail.

Now the elders chanted: *"Coth-cho! Coth-cho! Coth-cho!"*

A buffalo lumbered slowly toward the crowd of young braves. From its size, Poli judged it to be a calf.

At once the young braves leapt to their horses and circled the buffalo, jabbing at the air with their lances.

Chief Tosh-a-wah raised his hands and cried to the heavens: "Give us strength so that the buffalo may provide for us in our need!"

The braves brandished their lances, but they did not launch them. They circled the buffalo as if dancing.

Eagle Blood was at Poli's side, whispering: "*Coth-cho! Coth-cho!*"

"The buffalo gives us food and shelter, clothing and tools," Chief Tosh-a-wah declared. "He protects us from our enemies when he is a shield, and from the cold when he is a blanket."

"He shelters us from the rain when he is our tepee, and gives us drink when we thirst," Eagle Blood chanted. "From his hooves come our glue—and from his hair our rope!"

"All things come from the buffalo!" Chief Tosh-a-wah cried. "His horns and sinews are our weapons and strength, and wherever he goes we follow." He raised a lance high in the air. "If the Texans had kept out of our country, there might have been peace. Oh do not ask us to give up the buffalo for the sheep!"

The warriors' voices rose and Chief Tosh-a-wah flung the lance toward the circle of braves; the braves leapt to the ground, avoided the spear, charged the buffalo calf and tore at it with their hands.

Poli gasped, watched the buffalo skin rise in the

air, saw that two young boys were hiding beneath it.

"*Coth-cho! Coth-cho!*" the tribe chanted, and the young braves ran to Chief Tosh-a-wah and dropped the skin at his feet.

"Sometimes," Eagle Blood said, "we use such a skin to make our way into the midst of a large herd in order to lead it to our hunters."

Two young Comanches rode out onto the prairie, a long floppy object draped across the neck of one horse. The rider dropped the object to the ground.

"That's the dead Comanche," Chief Tosh-a-wah stated.

The dead Comanche was made from strips of braided buffalo skin; Chief Tosh-a-wah explained that this was a game all young braves had to master before they could take their places among the men of the tribe.

Two riders stood at a distance. One shouted and then the horses bolted forward. When the braves were nearly upon the dummy, the horses veered away from one another; as they passed to either side, each boy dropped into his loop and, with his free hand, reached for the dead Comanche. The horses did not slow down, and for several yards the dummy hung suspended in the air between them.

"Yi-yi—!" one of the boys cried, and then the boys sat upright on their horses, the dead Comanche once again draped across a pony's neck.

Eagle Blood explained to Poli that no Comanche warrior could, with honor, leave a comrade dead upon the battlefield, for the Comanches believed that the immortal spirit of a man lay in his scalp. If a dead warrior were not recovered, his spirit would never enter the spirit world.

"That's also why we never leave an enemy dead upon the battlefield without first taking *his* scalp," Eagle Blood said. "For in this way his spirit will be left in eternal torment."

Chief Tosh-a-wah nodded. "Men enter the spirit world in the same form they hold at the time of their passing," he said. "If an enemy were to take out the eyes of one of my sons, that son would wander without sight until the end of time."

When the braves had finished performing for their elders, Poli and Eagle Blood practiced together, and on the following day they worked as a team in front of the entire tribe. They shot across the prairie as if they were one horse and one rider. Poli kept his eyes upon the ground, a shade to the left of the place upon which Hermano's hooves were about to land, and when Eagle Blood turned his pinto away slightly, Poli did the same. When Eagle Blood dropped into his loop, Poli dropped into his own. He hung there, pressed against Hermano's side, Hermano's hooves spraying dirt upon him. Poli reached down with his free hand, watched Eagle Blood do the same, and an instant later the dead Comanche lay across Hermano's neck.

The young braves sent a piercing cry into the air. Poli rode with Eagle Blood to Chief Tosh-a-wah, who praised him and said that Poli was more than a Mexican.

Poli thanked Chief Tosh-a-wah. But when he said, proudly, that most Mexicans had Indian blood in them—that only Indians inhabited Mexico before the Spaniards came three centuries before—Chief Tosh-a-wah turned away without speaking.

Chapter 7

BLOOD BROTHERS

The Comanches left nothing behind them that was written down, but they used stones, bones, and sticks to make pictures in the earth, and they carved and painted pictures on the walls of caves. The deep vermillion paint they loved was made by pulverizing cinnabar—quicksilver ore—and mixing it with bear grease. Eagle Blood taught Poli how to make this paint, and how to read Comanche pictures.

Poli explained all this to his father when he returned to his camp with Eagle Blood.

"They make pictures on buffalo hides also," Poli said, "but the most important pictures are those they make on their bodies. Before battle, a Comanche warrior will write the legend of his life on his body so that his story will perish with his flesh and accompany him into the next life."

"Is there nothing you forget, my son?"

"If a man forgets, he's in danger of dying."

"And where did you learn that?"

"From Eagle Blood."

Suddenly, Señor Rodriguez grasped his son's arm and twisted it, palm up. There was a broad cut across Poli's left wrist.

"Did Eagle Blood give you that?" he asked.

"No. I gave it to myself. Eagle Blood did the same." Eagle Blood showed his cut to Señor Rodriguez and declared that by mixing blood he and Poli were brothers for life.

"And if the Comanches make war against the Texans, my son—what then?"

Poli tossed a stone into the Medina River and watched the ripples spread.

"If your father's right and Mexico makes war so it can get back the Republic of Texas, what will I do?"

"You'll do what's right," Eagle Blood said.

Poli picked up another stone and hurled it angrily.

"Your words are foolish," he said. "I'm a Mexican and my family's Mexican—I may be your brother, but I'm also my father's son. No matter which way I choose I'll hurt somebody. Didn't you *see* how angry my father was?"

"Yes."

"So how can I do what's right—when I may have to choose between two paths, each of which will *seem* to be right?"

"Sometimes a road may fork and both paths may lead you where you're going—"

"*Some*times . . ." Poli said.

He stared at the still water. Its gray surface looked like smooth, dusty metal. He imagined himself peeling strips of the metal from the river and rolling the strips into rifle barrels. The water's gray skin turned black; he imagined gliding on the water's surface all night long, south towards home, until the sun rose and shone upon the river—until the metal softened, melted . . .

When Señor Rodriguez called to them that it was time to eat, they rose.

"I wish I had answers for you that would help, but I see that I don't. Perhaps sometimes we come to a forking path and no matter which road we choose, we choose the wrong one." Eagle Blood paused. "What I think is this: Your father's angry because he's frightened."

"Of what?"

"When he looked at your wrist, that's what I thought—Poli's father is scared his son may be hurt."

"But what can I do? What would you do if you were in my place?"

Eagle Blood took Poli's hand in his own, so that the wounds on their wrists touched. "I would find a friend like you," he said.

As soon as they were by the campfire, their plates filled with grilled meat—the rabbit Poli had brought home—Señor Rodriguez asked Poli to tell him of all that had happened at the Comanche camp. His anger was gone, his eyes a clear soft brown, and so, while they ate, Poli told his father about the Loop and the dead

Comanches and the kind of hide-and-seek the Indians played in which Comanche boys covered themselves with dead grass so that they would look like small mounds—of how they could lie in the tall grass without moving, and of how they would sometimes wrap themselves in blankets so that from a distance they would appear to be boulders.

Poli told his father that he had begun to learn Comanche dialect and sign language: the smoke signals used by day and the fire signals used by night. He'd learned to imitate the sounds of animals, to follow trails through untracked territory, and to prepare *pemmican*, a food made of buffalo meat, bone marrow, and dried berries, and preserved in a tallow which came from boiled buffalo hooves. Because it could stay fresh for years, the Comanches carried *pemmican* on all their journeys.

Poli told his father of the wondrous uses to which the Comanches put the buffalo, how from the dung they made fuel, from the horns ladles, from the hair pillows and rope, from the blood paint, and from the boiled hooves glue. From the shoulder blades they fashioned axes and hoes, and from the hides they made robes, leggings, and shields. Nothing was wasted. The tail was employed for a fly whisk, and even the buffalo's long beard, for which he was sometimes called Uncle, was used: to make ornaments for their clothes.

Poli sat on the ground next to his bedroll, watching the stars, talking with Eagle Blood about how to understand the configurations in the heavens so they might guide one's travel at night, how to take account of their shifting movements at different times of the year. The Big Dipper was low on the horizon, as if, Poli thought, it were getting ready to scoop its harvest from the Earth.

Señor Rodriguez came and sat with them.

"I would have spoken earlier," Señor Rodriguez said, "but I didn't want to spoil the good news I had for you by mixing it with the anger I was feeling before."

"Then you've found a job?" Poli exclaimed.

"Yes. Tomorrow we can leave this camp behind and move into San Antonio. Not only have I found a job for myself, but I've been able to get you work too—as an apprentice for Mr. William Tivy, who's an excellent gunsmith."

"And you?"

"I'll work as a hand in the stables of Jim Goodman —he needs somebody who knows horses—and he also expects me to work with him as a guide. Jim's a land surveyor and prospector."

Señor Rodriguez had talked with many Mexicans while he was in San Antonio. One of them, Ambrosio Garza, a member of the city's council, promised to speak to the mayor, Samuel Maverick, about giving Señor Rodriguez the deed to land which all settlers in Texas were entitled to.

"If we care for the land, it becomes ours," Señor Rodriguez said. "Texas is going to be good to us, my son."

Land of their own! Poli wanted to leap and to dance. But when he turned to Eagle Blood and saw the sadness in Eagle Blood's eyes, his own happiness washed out of him. He did not want to take away his father's hopes, nor did he want to promise Eagle Blood that he would try to be somebody he could not be. Like his father, he believed in giving to the land so that it would give back; but then he thought of what Eagle Blood believed . . .

"Someday soon, Poli," his father said, "we'll have what we never had in Mexico: our own home on our own property."

"Yes," Poli said, and he felt his father's lips on his forehead.

Poli lay down. He said nothing to Eagle Blood. What could he say that would make a difference? Like the Comanches, he too wondered how it could be that anyone could *own* the land, even if one plowed it, tilled it, harrowed it, planted it, and worked it from sun-up until sundown, from season to season, from year to year, from generation to generation.

At dawn, Poli and Eagle Blood sat by the edge of the Medina.

"Today I'll go to San Antonio, and you'll head north," Poli said, "but what I wish is that I could be going with you."

"Yes."

"What I wish is that I could be free the way you are—free to travel where the buffalo travels, to set up a tepee anywhere at all and to call that place my home."

Poli threw a stone into the water. "When I was in Mexico I was a Mexican, and when I'm here I'm a Texan—part of one and part of the other. And should I stay away from Mexico forever I'd keep becoming less and less of a Mexican, yet you—no matter where you go, you're always a Comanche."

"Without our hunting grounds, though, we have nothing to eat or to trade or to use for our clothing and shelter. As my father says, Now the buffalo run like the brown sea, but soon the sea will turn to salt and our tongues will grow large with thirst."

Eagle Blood talked of what his father had told him: how the United Sates government was sending increasing numbers of Indians west onto Comanche hunting grounds; thus, the Comanches would have to fight against both these Indians and the Americans. His father had talked of the strength of the white man's armies; Eagle Blood himself had seen what Texans had already done to Comanche women and children.

"Some day my father will pass into the Spirit World and I'll lead my people. I don't want to be the leader of starving children and weeping mothers. Tomorrow I'll put feathers in my hair and go out to hunt with the men of the tribe, but when my father's no longer here, will I be able to lead my people as he has? Will I truly be my father's son?"

The questions, Poli knew, were like Tana-kawi's questions. Poli did not know how long he sat beside Eagle Blood in silence. His eyes were open, yet he felt as if he were asleep, dreaming of the different paths he and his brother would take, and of where they might lead.

Eagle Blood drew his knife, pointed to the river bank, where the grass moved. He crept silently along the water's edge, then parted the grass with the point of his blade.

The snake appeared suddenly, hissing and puffing itself up. Eagle Blood took a step backwards and raised his knife.

"No!" Poli cried, and he grabbed Eagle Blood's wrist.

The snake puffed and spread, as if to strike, but when Poli stretched out his hand toward it, it rolled over as if it were dead.

Poli lifted it, holding it behind the head with finger and thumb. It was nearly three feet long.

"It's only a hog-nosed snake," Poli said. "It eats toads. In Zaragosa we used to capture them and keep them in cages as pets."

Chapter 8

THE COUNCIL HOUSE FIGHT

When Señor Rodriguez was away on surveying trips, working as a mule packer and guide, Poli slept alone in the straw-thatched *jacal* he and his father had built in Bandera County, by the edge of Privilege Creek.

The land, halfway between San Antonio and Val Verde, was leased to Señor Rodriguez by the San Antonio City Council. Poli and his father had built their *jacal* on a small treeless plain that bordered the creek, the plain bounded on the south by gently sloping hills, on the east by the creek, and on the north and northwest by a steep hill covered with red cedar. Beyond the hill were forests of oak and dogwood, the forests alive with wild animals: bobcat, turkey, partridge, antelope, white-tailed deer, raccoons, and bear.

Along the creek, nut and fruit trees were plentiful: pecan and walnut, persimmon and plum. The *jacal*—a single-room, single-story square building with low, wide windows—resembled those Poli had known in

Zaragosa, though it was larger and sturdier, and Poli loved the hours and days he and his father worked together—clearing the land, building their home, hunting for game, storing firewood and food, salting away meat. While they worked side by side, time itself, like morning mists upon the river, seemed to float upwards, dissolve, and disappear.

And when his father was gone, Poli would come home in early evening and wander through the cool rich forest, listening for the rustling of small animals in the leaves and the flickering noises of birds; at these times he felt hopeful about everything. In such a beautiful and peaceful place, how could a man *not* be happy . . .

Poli would arrive at Bill Tivy's gunsmith shop shortly after sunrise, work until the midday siesta, and then again, after siesta, until suppertime. Bill was a knowledgeable and kind man, gruff at times, but fair, and he did not condescend to Poli either because he was a boy or a Mexican. He taught Poli to repair flintlocks, to rifle gun barrels, to fix pepperboxes on pistols, to grind and mix gunpowder, to trim stocks, tighten mainsprings, and mend firing pins. When Poli was through working on the guns and rifles—usually in late afternoon—he would sharpen knives, swords, and lances. He was content enough while he was working, but mostly he longed for the hours spent away from town—alone, or with his father, or with Eagle Blood.

In late fall, their hunt over, Eagle Blood's band of Comanches returned to its camp by the Medina, and often Poli rode out and stayed with his friend, learning more and more about the Comanche ways and language. Poli and Eagle Blood hunted together, ate together, and slept side by side—sometimes outside Chief Tosh-a-wah's tepee and sometimes in the *jacal* at Privilege Creek. They explored Poli's forest, gathering food, herbs and nuts, calling to the animals, hunting them, and playing games with one another in which they practiced the skills which would soon make Eagle Blood a warrior of his tribe.

Sometimes Eagle Blood set out into the forest first, and twenty minutes later Poli would have to trail and find him—and at other times Eagle Blood would trail Poli. The two boys dug trenches and covered themselves with leaves; they climbed trees and dropped from limbs onto one another's back; they wrestled and they shot at each other with blunt-tipped arrows and they lassoed one another with their lariats. They cooked their meals from the animals they killed and from the herbs, nuts, berries, and fruit they gathered. At night they often slept on the forest floor, their weapons beside them, the hooting of owls passing through their dreams like the sounds of distant trains.

During the previous year, Comanche tribes had raided many local settlements in and around San Antonio, killing women and children, taking captives. In retaliation, Mirabeau Buonaparte Lamar, who had succeeded Sam Houston as president of the Republic of Texas, ordered the Texas Army to take control of all land to the upper waters of the Rio Grande; in this effort he enlisted the help of the Lipan, Tonkawa, and Mescalero Indians. His stated aim was nothing less than to exterminate or to drive from Texas—forever—all Comanches.

In addition, as Poli learned from Chief Tosh-a-wah, increasing numbers of Indians—Shawnee, Delaware, Kickapoo, Seminole, and Cherokee—were being uprooted from the east and forced by the United States government to settle on traditional Comanche hunting grounds.

Alarmed by Comanche raids, the people of San Antonio organized their own defense forces, which they put under the command of Captain Jack Hays. They named the first division of these forces the Texas Rangers. At the same time, Mayor Maverick sent a petition to the capital in Austin, demanding that the Republic of Texas take measures to protect townspeople and settlers in the San Antonio region from looting and raiding.

Because Chief Tosh-a-wah's tribe had remained at peace with San Antonians, the townspeople did not take out their frustrations or rage on Poli. Still, they were wary, and each day Poli could sense their coldness and their fear.

Early in 1840, the government of Texas responded to Mayor Maverick's petition, sending Colonel William S. Fisher to San Antonio with three companies of Texas troops. Colonel Fisher soon learned of Poli's friendship with Eagle Blood's tribe, and came to him with a new job offer: to serve as his interpreter. And when, a week later, Colonel Henry Karnes met with chieftains from Comanche bands that roamed the far reaches of the Texas Republic and announced that he had reached an agreement with them to gather for a peace conference in San Antonio, Poli was thrilled.

"The Bible does not say that the wolf and the lamb must love one another," Señor Rodriguez said to his son, after Poli gave him his news. "It only says that they shall lie down *alongside* one another."

Several days after Poli accepted his new commission, President Lamar dispatched Adjutant General Hugh McLeod to negotiate a treaty in San Antonio on behalf of the Republic of Texas.

Thus, on March 19, 1840, a year after Poli first crossed the Rio Grande, he and his father stood and watched from the steps of the San Antonio Court House as sixty-five Comanches, including twelve chiefs, rode into the town's center.

When Poli saw Chief Tosh-a-wah approach, his heart swelled. Chief Tosh-a-wah's face was streaked boldly in lines of red and black, and he wore a lone eagle feather in his scalplock. The other chiefs were dressed as if for war: their faces daubed with paint, their body hair plucked out, colorful ribbons tied to the tails of their horses. Their lances were painted red, their shields trimmed with feathers, animal teeth, and scalps. They wore elaborate headdresses made of buffalo horn and deer antler; one chief wore a headdress fashioned from a stuffed white crane.

The citizens of San Antonio lined the road that led from Soledad Street to Military Plaza and gaped at the fantastic entourage. The faces of the Indian women were painted also, in bright reds, blues, and blacks, and the children rode with the women. Between the chiefs and the other Indians, a warrior on foot led a horse, and on the horse, in Indian clothing, rode a single white woman.

On either side of the Court House—known to San Antonians as the Council House—companies of San Antonio volunteers stood at attention: the Mexicans under General Seguin and the Texans under Jack Hays.

The Indians reached the Council House and dismounted. The chiefs moved forward; they were not, despite the markings on their faces, the war chiefs of the Comanche tribes but the civil leaders—the peace chiefs—and Poli immediately pointed this out to Colonel Karnes.

"We'll see about that," Colonel Karnes said, and he opened the door to the Council House so that the Indian chiefs might enter.

"Be careful," Señor Rodriguez said. He touched Poli's shoulder, then left.

Karnes and McLeod took seats on one side of a table, alongside Colonel Fisher. Two soldiers stood by the door, their rifles at the ready.

Without ceremony, General McLeod began: "According to the terms of our agreement, you were to

bring your white captives in with you. Where are they?"

Poli translated, and Chief Muguara went to the door and signalled. The white woman who had been riding with the Comanches entered the courthouse chamber, her eyes downcast. Poli saw that her face was scarred hideously in broad crescent slashes, the tip of her nose burned away.

McLeod turned to Poli. "Tell that damned red devil they promised to bring in thirteen captives and we want to know where they are and we want to know *now!*"

Again Poli translated. Chief Muguara replied angrily that the woman, Matilda Lockhart, was the sole captive. He turned to the other chiefs and asked if they had any whites living with their tribes; they all said they did not.

"This is a goddamned farce," Karnes whispered to McLeod. "We know they've got more and all they want is to bring 'em in one at a time so they can get better terms each time they do. I say to hell with 'em."

"I have lived with Chief Tosh-a-wah's tribe," Poli said. "I can vouch for what he says—there have never been any white captives in his camp."

"Maybe not," McLeod said. "But there are other chiefs and tribes and we know for sure they've got 'em. You tell your chiefs that I say this to them: They haven't come here to make peace."

Poli told the Indians what McLeod said.

"If we had come to make war," Chief Tosh-a-wah replied, "would we have brought with us our women and our children? That is our sign of peace and of trust."

While Poli translated Chief Tosh-a-wah's words, Karnes hardly paid attention. Instead, he whispered that the chance was one that might not come again. "When else are we ever gonna get twelve of these devils in one place at the same time?"

"But they're telling the truth," Poli protested. "Chief Tosh-a-wah doesn't lie—these men are the peace chiefs of their tribes, not the war chiefs. In the Comanche councils, the peace chiefs are the ones who decide whether or not—"

"You speak when you're spoken to, boy," Karnes snapped, "or we'll take you for one of these double-eyed rascals. You hear what I'm telling you?"

"I hear," Poli said. "But I beg of you—"

"Soldier," Karnes ordered, ignoring Poli. "Send the others in now!"

A soldier opened the door, barked out a command, and two dozen uniformed men of the Texas Army entered, their guns drawn. They surrounded the Indian chiefs.

Karnes, McLeod, and Fisher stood behind the table, side by side, their backs to the far wall, their pistols pointed at the chiefs.

"Okay, son," Karnes said to Poli. "Now you listen up and get this straight and don't pull none of your sneaking Injun tricks. You tell these devils that we have a deal to make and it's the best one they're gonna get. You tell them we'll let one chief go and that we're gonna hold the others. For every white captive they bring in, we'll let another chief go. That's fair, ain't it? And when

we have all our captives back, *then* we'll sit down in
one of their damned powwows and talk about a peace
treaty."

Poli looked toward Chief Tosh-a-wah and was
silent.

Chief Tosh-a-wah nodded and spoke: "I know
every stream and every wood between the Rio Grande
and the Arkansas," he stated. "I have hunted and lived
over that country for many years. When the game beats
away from us, we pull down our tepees and move off,
leaving no trace, and so in a while it returns. But the
white man comes and cuts down the trees, building
houses and fences so that the buffalo become frightened and leave and never return and we are left to starve.
And if we choose to follow the thin buffalo trails, we
must make our camps on the hunting grounds of other
tribes so that there is not enough food for any of us.
Then war comes and does not go away."

Chief Tosh-a-wah stopped speaking as abruptly as
he had begun.

Poli translated his words, but McLeod only grunted
in response. "Ask him about the captives," he said. "Tell
him we don't care about his damned buffalo. And if
these Indians want to kill one another, that's fine with
us too. Saves the government money and soldiers."

"When I heard that the Texan wanted to talk peace,"
Chief Tosh-a-wah continued, "I felt glad as the ponies
do when the fresh grass rises from the land in the begin-
ning of the year. But now—" he pointed to the soldiers,
and then to the document that Karnes held in his hand

"—now I see that the Texan tries to make peace with honey-talk, with white man's paper-that-talks-two-ways."

Poli translated. "Just tell them what I said," McLeod ordered. "I ain't interested in the rest."

"But if I do that," Poli said, "they'll fight. You know that—!"

McLeod pointed his gun at Poli and cocked the hammer.

"You tell them, boy, and tell them fast!"

Poli translated McLeod's words. Chief Muguara cried out that there were no other captives. The other chiefs shouted their assent; the chief who wore the head-dress with the white crane stepped forward. He pointed a finger at McLeod.

"So how do you like our answer?" he asked in English.

McLeod's face turned red. "Put the shackles on that lying bastard!" he commanded.

"No!" Poli cried. "No!"

A soldier was already moving toward the chief. Poli stepped in front of the chief, to stop the soldier, but the soldier bashed Poli across the forehead with the butt-end of his rifle.

Poli fell to the floor. He tried to rise, but was hit again. Warm liquid ran down his cheek. He saw the flash of a knifeblade, and then, just above his head, he heard the crashing sound of a gunblast.

Poli wiped the blood from his face and watched a Comanche chief topple forward, blood spurting from an opening in his chest. The chief covered the opening

with his hands—another shot tore the air—and Poli
watched the chief's fingers disappear in an explosion
of blood.

Chief Muguara wrestled a gun from a Texas soldier and began shooting. Poli reached to his hip for his
bowie knife, but a soldier smashed Poli's hand with his
boot. The Indian chiefs were shouting—war cries, cries
for help from the warriors outside the Council House,
cries for their women and children to flee—and the soldiers were firing and reloading at close range. Poli tried
to rise again; he looked up and saw a soldier's wide
astonished eyes and realized that the soldier's lower jaw
had been shot away—and then something struck him
from behind. It was as if water were closing above, and
he felt himself going under, downwards toward something black and awful.

Poli reached to his forehead and felt the damp clot-
ted blood.

"Don't move," Señor Rodriguez said. "You're not
hurt badly, but you must rest—"

Poli heard gunblasts and shouts. "I have to warn
Eagle Blood," he said, and he tried to sit up.

The room tilted to one side; Poli saw Chief Muguara
lying across the body of a young soldier. Both were dead.
Another soldier sat against the wall while blood poured
from the place in which his eye had once been. Poli
stared at a young soldier's face and realized it looked
curious because the scalp, from the top of the forehead
to the back of the skull, was gone. "I told them not

to," Poli began. "I begged General McLeod—"

"Come," Señor Rodriguez said, lifting his son. "Come, Poli. We'll leave by the back door and ride out to Privilege Creek, where we'll be safe. Lean on me—"

Poli let his father lead him to the rear of the Council House. He drew deep breaths of air into his lungs, felt his head begin to clear. He knew his father would try to keep him from entering the square, so as he felt his strength return he pretended weakness.

"Hermano is tied to a tree over there—"

Poli walked with his father, but when his father let go of him for Poli to mount Hermano, the boy broke away and ran back toward the Council House.

"Poli! No—!"

Poli kept running. He stopped at the side of a fallen Texas Ranger, took the Ranger's rifle, and ran around to the front of the Council House. On its steps was a dead Indian child, a knife in its breast. Beside the child, his hat between the two bodies, lay Judge Thompson, a tomahawk protruding from the back of his black suit.

People ran through the square as if crazed. Indians, women, soldiers, children—they ran and they moaned and they shrieked and they cried out for mercy. Men lay dying in the sun, calling for help—calling for water, for their mothers, for God. An Indian passed by, shooting at soldiers as he rode, a broken lance embedded in his hip as if it were a bullfighter's banderilla.

At the western edge of the town square, Texas soldiers squatted in two ragged lines and fired into a stone house to the south; from inside the stone house, the

Comanches returned the rifle fire with arrows. Suddenly
a soldier appeared on the roof, a flaming torch in his
hand. He let the torch drop down the chimney, then
jumped away. Within a few seconds, the Comanches
fled the blazing building; as they did, the soldiers
gunned them down without mercy.

A warrior galloped past, his lance poised in the
air, then suddenly tumbled from his horse, dead. Poli
did not hesitate. He mounted the horse and turned in
a circle. A few feet to the west of Council House—his
chest a mass of blood and flesh, his eyes staring straight
into the sun—lay Chief Tosh-a-wah.

Poli spurred the horse and rode from the square.
Behind the Council House the dead were quiet. Poli
did not see his father, but Hermano was still there. Poli
changed mounts and started south.

When Poli reached the hill overlooking Eagle
Blood's camp, he stopped. The women were wailing
and gashing themselves with knives and arrows. The
young braves Poli had played with so often had cut their
hair short and slashed themselves on their arms and
chests. The news had already arrived. Poli walked slowly
down the hill. Even as they mourned, the Comanches
were taking down their tepees.

Poli walked to the tepee he knew well, and inside
he found Eagle Blood and Tana-kawi. There was a hatred
in Eagle Blood's eyes that Poli had never before seen,
and that hatred, intended for all white men forever, was
now meant for Poli too. He said nothing. He stood still,

wanting to comfort Eagle Blood—to let him know that his heart was breaking too. But he knew there were no words to ease the pain for his brother, just as there would be no words to ease his pain on the day his own father would be taken away.

Eagle Blood closed his eyes, opened them; the hatred was gone. Poli left the tepee and waited outside.

He stayed with Eagle Blood's tribe all that day and through the night. When Chief Tosh-a-wah and the others were brought into the camp, the howling of the women, warriors, and children increased and rose to the stars, and when the stars faded and the sun showed itself in the pale morning sky, Eagle Blood buried his father by the Medina River. On the grave he slaughtered his father's horse so that, as the Comanches believed, the great chief would not have to walk when he was in the spirit world.

Thirty-two Comanches had been killed. Among the dead were three women, two children, and all twelve chieftains. Twenty-seven other Comanches, mostly women and children, were being held prisoner.

Late that morning Eagle Blood said farewell to his brother and departed for the north. Poli stood by the Medina until he could no longer see the departing tribe, or the cloud of dust that accompanied them.

Chapter 9

A SLAVE NO MORE

Poli did not see Eagle Blood again for nearly two years. Then, in late February of 1842, after his thirteenth birthday, he decided to search out his friend. He made inquiries and headed north along the San Saba, locating Eagle Blood's camp some seventy miles from San Antonio.

Many of the tribe's warriors were ill, others had left and joined small bands of raiders. To hunt the buffalo, which roamed farther and farther south, Eagle Blood said that his weakened tribe would have to fight against other Indians, and he neither wanted to fight nor believed he had the strength to prevail.

Poli told Eagle Blood he had lost his job after the Council House fight and now stayed on the land at Privilege Creek, living from its bounty and selling what was left over—game, vegetables, fruits—in the San Antonio market.

The young men were glad to be together—cooking,

riding, hunting; still, Poli perceived a sadness in Eagle Blood's eyes that made his own heart heavy.

One evening at the start of Poli's second week with Eagle Blood, a scout rode into the camp, his horse lathered, looking for Poli.

"The Mexican Army invaded San Antonio this morning," he said. "The Texans have fled."

"My father—?" Poli asked.

"He's waiting for you at home."

"Has he joined with the army?"

"With which army?"

Poli stopped. "I don't know," he said, and he looked to Eagle Blood.

"I will help you prepare for the journey home," Eagle Blood said.

"Your father told me to warn you to be careful when you return. When either side finds a Mexican riding alone, they assume the rider is an enemy."

"Is my father alone?"

"Yes. But it's safer for him where he is—outside of town. Most of the Mexican soldiers are in San Antonio, and whenever they find Mexicans by themselves, they either force them into service or kill them."

"So what will you do now, my friend?" Eagle Blood asked, while Poli packed his gear. "Will you fight with your Mexican brothers against Texas? And if you do, and if Texas regains its land, will Texas regard *all* Mexicans as their enemies? What will you do?"

Eagle Blood turned away and walked ten steps, then
turned back, and Poli could see that Eagle Blood now
feared for him, even as he had feared for Eagle Blood.

About five miles from San Antonio, Poli cut southwards from the San Saba, through the thin forests that
lined the Medina, so as to avoid the town itself. In his
mind was only one thought—to find his father before
the Mexican Army did.

He left the Medina, travelled an old Penateka trail
toward Privilege Creek, and dismounted. He was less
than a mile from home, but he wanted to be careful,
so as not to fall into a trap that would threaten both
his father and himself.

He bent over to drink from the river, but stopped:
In the tula grass to his right, a few yards off, a shape
moved and the shape was not that of an animal. Poli
drew his knife, dropped to his knees, circled quietly,
then moved forward again. The shape scurried away.
Poli watched sunlight glance from the barrel of a gun.
A Texan fleeing from the Mexicans? A Mexican soldier
cut off from his army?

Suddenly the gun barrel swung toward him and
Poli did not hesitate. He took a step to his right, then
dove through the air, bringing the weight of his body
crashing down upon the arm which held the gun. The
gun skittered through the grass, toward the river bank.

Poli locked his arm around his would-be assailant's
throat, stuck his bowie knife into his ribs.

"Talk and talk fast," Poli said.

But the throat he held, he saw, was neither that of a Texan nor a Mexican; it was coal black, damp with sweat.

"Hey now, Poli," the boy said. "Hey you let me go now, hey—"

Poli dragged the boy a few feet, retrieved the gun, put it into his own right hand, and turned the boy around.

"It's me—Seth Turnbow. You know me and I know you." The black boy rubbed his neck. "You sure got strong arms. Ain't no molasses in you."

Poli stared at the boy: Seth Turnbow, a thin boy about his own age, a Negro slave to one of the new American families that had settled in San Antonio during the previous year.

Poli did not lower the gun. "What are you doing on my land, and what do you know about my father?"

"Going down to Mexico," Seth said.

"My father?"

"Don't know. Maybe. I mean I'm the one going down to Mexico. It be why I'm here."

"Have you seen my father?"

"Ain't seen nobody but me and you."

"Why are you here?"

"You ain't gonna use that pistol now, are you?" Seth shivered. "I never did nothin' to you. I like you, Poli. We ain't got no fights never—"

"Just answer my question: What are you doing on my land? Talk!"

"Told you. Going down to Mexico. My mother and me belongs to Massah Brown, like you know, but the Mexicans kill him dead and my mother too. She gone to where you don't never come back from. So I be going to Mexico. Don't want to be a slave no more. I seen my chance." He dropped to his knees, clasping his hands in prayer. "Believe me now, Poli. Please believe me. I never did nothin' to you. Please—"

Poli stuck the gun into his belt and ordered Seth to rise. Seth would not look into Poli's eyes.

"Before she die, my mother told me to stay with Miz Brown no matter what, but I heared they don't allow no slaves down in Mexico, less the Indians get you, so I going there if you let me."

"It's all right," Poli said. "Come on. Come home with me. We'll see if my father's there."

Seth tugged on Poli's arm. "If you let me go down to Mexico, I'll be your friend. I'll give you things. I'll give you anything you want." He searched in his pockets, and found a single gold coin.

With trembling fingers, he offered it to Poli.

"It be all I've got but it's yours if you let me go down to Mexico."

"Put away your money and come," Poli said. "You'll need food, water, and rest for the journey."

Poli fetched Hermano, then walked with Seth toward his home.

"Do you know how far it is to Mexico?" Poli asked.

"It's far," Seth said. "But if the Mexico Army come all the way from there and folks like you did too once, then I figger I can get all the way down there."

"But we came from there because we were slaves too," Poli said.

"But not like here."

They stopped at a small stand of live oak, from which Poli surveyed the scene at Privilege Creek. He saw no movement near his home. On the plain east of the straw-thatched house, his father's horses grazed peacefully.

Suddenly Seth turned and lifted his torn shirt. "You look here, Poli, so you know how true I've been talking to you. You look here."

Poli looked and saw the long wide scars on the boy's back, some of them raw and open.

"Massah Brown, he ain't gonna whip me no more, where he be now. The Mexico soldiers fix him good.

That's why I be going down there now, if you let me. He whip my mother worse than me but she won't feel that sting now. Don't want to be a slave no more, Poli. In Texas or nowhere. I seen my chance. I seen it."

Señor Rodriguez was at home, and he and Poli tended to Seth's wounds, then put the boy to sleep on the floor next to Poli's bedroll. In the morning, however, when Poli awoke, Seth was gone, along with the pistol, two water bags, ammunition, and one of Señor Rodriguez's horses.

The Mexican army, under General Vasquez, withdrew from San Antonio, and the region was tranquil all through the spring and summer. Then, on September 11, 1842, a force of twelve hundred Mexicans, under General Adrian Woll, entered the city. What was left of the Texas militia fled, as did most of the town's citizens. The Mexican army secured San Antonio, leaving a small detachment to guard it, and camped by Salado Creek.

But this time Sam Houston had a plan. Several thousand soldiers of the Texas army rapidly joined with the local militia; together they drove Woll's army back into the abandoned city, trapped it there, and laid siege to the city.

During the siege, many of the town's Mexican families stayed with Poli and his father at Privilege Creek. A few Mexicans had joined the Texas volunteers fighting with General Somervell, but most, like Poli's father, chose not to take sides—either for the nation they were born in, or for the nation in which they had settled.

One young Mexican, Garcia Fontanez, tried to rally the others to volunteer for Somervell's army with him; Garcia's father heard of his son's plans, however, captured him, and tied him to a tree.

"But we're Texans now!" Garcia cried out. "We're Texans!"

"Yes. And our brothers, sisters, mothers, and fathers are still in Mexico—and in San Antonio your beloved Texans call you 'dirty Mex'—"

"I was born in Texas!" Garcia cried out. "And I will live here and die here if I must. Only set me free! Set me free so that I may lead others to fight for Texas!"

Poli sat by the campfire with his father, listening to Garcia's cries, and to the arguments of the men. Some of them blamed Mexico, since it had crossed the border and invaded Texas, while others blamed the United States government, since it encouraged Americans to settle in Texas and provided the Texans with military and financial aid. What choice did the Mexican government have? As long as Texas was an independent republic, Mexico might be relatively safe, but if Texas became part of the United States, what then? The United States seemed intent on expanding forever—north toward Canada, west to California and Oregon, south to the Gulf of Mexico. Why would its expansion stop at the Rio Grande?

In the middle of the fourth night of the siege, Garcia freed himself from the tree, stole his father's gun, shot him, armed himself, and fled from the camp.

At the sound of gunshots, the men woke. Poli ran with them, only to find that Garcia's father was dead. Now, Poli thought, it begins again. Now the poison infects from within. Now, like fish crazed with hunger, we begin to feed upon ourselves. He mounted Hermano and, with a dozen others, he sped along the trail to San Antonio. When they reached the edge of the town, however, they were told by Texas soldiers that Garcia had slipped through their lines and found sanctuary within the walls of Fort San Antonio—as a new volunteer for the Mexican forces of General Woll. As his father had warned when he tied Garcia to a tree, Garcia was deceiving them all along—he was only trying to entrap others, to lure them to their deaths. Poli and his small band turned around and began the bitter journey home.

They travelled through the lines of General Somervell's army, watching the soldiers of the Texas army wake and prepare for battle: cleaning and oiling their guns, sharpening their knives, stacking ammunition, tending to their horses.

Suddenly a shot rang out and Hermano reared into the air. A second shot sprayed dirt onto Poli's legs. The Texas soldiers laughed. Poli slipped his rifle from his shoulder, let it rest in the crook of his arm.

"Are you a Mexican or a Texan?" a soldier shouted.

Poli glanced ahead and saw a line of Texas soldiers waiting for them, their pistols ready, the firing hammers cocked.

"Let us pass," Poli said. "We mean no harm. Garcia

Fontanez has killed his father. We—"

"Glad to hear it," the soldier said. "Because if you ask me, the best Mexican's a dead one, just like your damned Injun friends. I know you, boy. I remember you from when you fought with the Comanches."

"I didn't fight," Poli replied calmly. "I tried to bring peace. All we ask is to return to our families—we didn't come to fight against you."

"But you didn't come to answer my question either, and by God, you're gonna! Are you Texans or Mexicans? Come on and tell us—!"

"Texans!" one of the older Mexicans called out, proudly. "We are Texans!"

"Then why ain't you here fighting with us, you yellow-backed Mexican coward!"

The soldier's gun swiveled, aimed now for the old Mexican's chest, and when it did, Poli leapt from Hermano, landed broadside on the soldier, and knocked his gun away. Poli jabbed the point of his knife against the soldier's throat.

Others closed in swiftly.

"Don't shoot!" the soldier cried. "Hold your fire!"

Poli pressed on the blade, so that a thin line of blood slid along the man's throat.

"Please!" the soldier cried out. "Let the others go. Please—"

"Are you afraid to die for Texas?" Poli asked. "*Are* you?"

The circle of soldiers broke. Jack Hays stood above Poli, his gun resting in his holster.

"You let the soldier go, Poli, and we'll let you and your friends get on back home."

"Yes. Only first this soldier will say that we're not cowards."

"These men have had some hard times," Hays said. "They've seen the way the Mexicans butchered their brothers when they took 'em prisoner. They'll fight anybody who's against 'em, and anybody who's not for 'em, and neither you nor me is gonna be able to keep the killing away from your door neither. Not forever, Poli."

Two days later, after the sounds of cannon were quiet for more than twelve hours, Poli journeyed back to town. When he reached the spot where he had spoken with Hays, the soldiers were gone. And when he entered San Antonio, he found that the Mexicans had departed also. An old *campesino*, foraging for food and supplies in the rubble, told Poli that Woll's Army had retreated towards Mexico, Somervell in pursuit. Texas would remain a free republic yet a while longer.

The streets of San Antonio, however, were deserted and in ruins—buildings torn apart by cannonballs, stores and homes burned to the ground. Poli could hear his father's voice, reciting an old saying: They make a desert and call it peace. The stench of death hung in the air like foul-smelling moss. Poli rode to Military Plaza, where the bodies of soldiers of the Mexican army, bloated and fly-covered, were piled high, one upon the other—grotesque pyramids of mutilated flesh and severed limbs.

Their faces masked, men loaded the rotting corpses onto wagons. Poli got down from his horse, tied a bandanna around his nose and mouth. All day long and into the night he worked with the other men, carrying the bodies from town, digging long and deep graves, laying the dead in, covering them with earth.

When the last spadeful of earth had been shoveled in, and the last prayer said, Poli mounted his horse and returned to Privilege Creek.

Chapter 10

RETURN TO MEXICO

Not long after peace came to the region, Eagle Blood's tribe camped once again on their old site by the Medina. Eagle Blood was now a full-fledged warrior, and on their first day together, he told his brother the story of his initiation.

The previous summer, just past his own thirteenth birthday, he went off into the woods by himself for four days and nights, carrying with him a buffalo robe, a bone pipe, tobacco, and materials for lighting the pipe.

He took with him neither horse nor food, weapons nor medicine. Dressed in only a breechclout and moccasins, he walked many miles, stopping four times each day to pray; then, on an isolated hill he stopped and waited, and neither ate nor drank until the spirits visited him and gave to him the *puha*—that power which could transform him into a man and a warrior.

"I saw a great eagle," he told Poli, "and the eagle devoured an entire buffalo and became so large that its wings covered the sun and put out the light of the world. The eagle came again in the night and it found the owl and it ate the owl. Then it carried away the young of the owl and dropped them from a great height in the sky, so that they were crushed. I heard thunder and I watched the eagle wrap its wings around the moon and make the night as black as the day already was.

"I looked down and a snake was entwined between my legs. In the snake's mouth was a single eagle feather. I held the snake, lifting it to the heavens, and the moon appeared again, like a lake of snow in a black forest. I wrestled with the snake until daybreak and when it hissed the eagle flew away from the sun and light came to the world again.

"I returned to my tribe and my name was still Eagle Blood, but the eagle, which has great power in war and hangs from our hair and our shields when we go into battle, had become my own enemy, so that when I see an eagle feather now I must look the other way. And when an eagle is killed I may not eat of its flesh or I will die also. It is the snake, which hides in the ground, who carries my power now. When the eagle eats, it does not like anything to be behind it. It twists its head all around as it tears at flesh. It is the snake alone that can steal the eagle's food so that the eagle will not kill the buffalo.

"I told the elders of my tribe of all I had seen and they told me my vision was proof that I was the one chosen to keep our tribe from starving. I was my father's son. When other men come to take our land from us, and kill our buffalo, we must now use the cunning and swiftness of the snake to defeat them. Often, like the snake, we must learn to strike before they do—while they sleep, and while they eat, and while they raise up their young. We must raid, or we will starve."

Raid or starve. Poli heard these words often from Eagle Blood and from the other warriors, and though he did not argue with his brother, he feared for him. He rode out frequently to Eagle Blood's camp, and took pride in seeing Eagle Blood become the leader of his people. But when he returned home he worried, not only about the fate of Eagle Blood and his tribe, but about the changes taking place within his brother's heart. Poli hoped Eagle Blood would one day soar again like the great bird for whom he had been named. A warrior as brave and true as Eagle Blood, he believed, should not draw his power from an animal that lived in shadows and survived by deceit.

San Antonio itself was a virtual ghost town now, its population, which had risen to over two thousand before the Vasquez invasion, dropping below five hundred. The armies of Texas and Mexico were weakened, and though Texans sometimes raided towns in northern Mexico and Mexicans raided towns in southern Texas, neither was prepared for a full-scale invasion. Both sides felt too weak to win, yet too bitter and fearful to stop fighting.

Terrified of reprisals from Texans, most Mexican families did not return to what was left of their homes, and few new American settlers were willing to brave the dangers of coming to a region scarred by the plundering, looting, and killing practiced by all, whether Mexican, Texan, or Indian.

Early in 1844, however, word reached San Antonio that others—from across the sea—were less fearful. A society called the *Adelsverein* had been formed in Germany and in July, 1844, after landing at Galveston, its members journeyed north and entered San Antonio.

Poli was there. He stood on the Council House steps with others, eager to get a glimpse of the strange-looking man he had heard about, a man who rode into town accompanied by a unit of Texas Rangers.

"There he is!" somebody yelled.

Captain Jack Hays, in his midnight-blue uniform and white Stetson hat, his sword held upright in a white-gloved fist, led the procession. Behind him, on a magnificent cream-colored roan, rode a man in a black velvet hat. In the hat was a long grey feather; under the hat the man's brown curls fell softly to his shoulders. He wore a black velvet collar on top of a grey wool blouse, the sun flashing brightly from the silver buttons of his blouse. Across his chest was a sash of black and gold silk, and from the sash hung a sword, its hilt embossed with silver curlicues. His black leather riding boots came above his knees. As he rode he inclined his head to left and to right, while behind him cavalrymen followed in two lines, swords at their sides.

"He sure is a sight in that hat!" Dick Howard exclaimed.

Poli and his father, who had come into town with Dick that morning, agreed.

"Well," a man in front of them said. "I don't reckon Hays's Stetson looks any too familiar to the king."

"He's not a king," Poli said. "He's a prince. Prince Solms-Braunfels, the cousin of Emperor William of Prussia and the friend of Prince Albert of England."

"If you say it, I believe it," Dick Howard said.

Others turned to Poli and he told them what he had learned: that the Prince had already met with Sam Houston in Austin and received the rights to land northeast of San Antonio, on the Comal River. Although the prince had only fifty settlers with him now, more would soon be arriving from Germany.

"I thought San Antonio was a town for Texans!" one man said, and others grunted their assent.

"Yes," Poli said. "But Mexicans have been here longer than Americans or Texans. San Antonio was established more than a hundred years ago as a mission to the Indians by Mexican priests."

"You're still foreigners to me," the man shot back. "And we'd all be a hell of a lot better off if you'd never come north in the first place."

Poli clenched the handle of his knife and moved toward the man, but Dick Howard grasped Poli by the shoulder.

"Hold on, Poli," he said quietly. "Go slow now."

Poli turned away.

"If you're so smart, Poli," Dick asked, "tell me this: What do they call that big pillow the prince is riding on?"

Poli looked at the gold silk which puffed out from the prince's saddle. He searched his mind for the correct military term, but could not find it. "I don't know," he said.

"That, Poli my boy," Dick said, "is what we old soldiers call the seat of the kingdom!"

While Señor Rodriguez and the other men laughed, Dick put his arm around Poli and led him from the crowd.

"I just wanted to ease things a bit," he said. "No point your getting into trouble for the likes of mean-spirited bastards like Grogan."

Poli and Dick watched the procession. Behind the Texas Rangers came the remainder of Prince Solms-Braunfels's retinue: barons and counts riding fine horses and wearing silks, velvets, and extravagant plumed hats; and then, on mules, other Germans—men, women, children, and servants, poor and tired-looking for the most part, who nevertheless smiled and waved to the onlookers.

Poli liked Dick Howard, and trusted him. Dick was thirty-one years old, a tall man with a barrel chest and a deep raspy voice that made him sound as if he were much older than his years. He had once been a West Point cadet, though why he had left and why he was not an officer in the United States Army were questions nobody ever asked him. Dick lived by himself in a small shack near the San Saba. He was the best surveyor and guide in San Antonio and a good friend to Señor Rodriguez.

"Poli's right about the other Germans who'll be here soon," Dick said to Poli and his father while the three men watched the parade go by. "I'm in charge of a party that's going to survey land for them—it's why I wanted to be sure you were here today."

Dick's tongue moved inside his right cheek the way it often did when he had something important on his mind; it was as if, Poli thought, he was searching for the taste of something he had once known and loved.

"I could use some good men and I'd like to have both of you come with me."

Poli looked toward his father.

"No," Señor Rodriguez said. "I haven't worked as a guide for almost a year now. I'm becoming too old to go out on the trail, Dick. And too slow. Besides, I have other plans, a different journey in mind."

"And you?"

"I'll stay with my father," Poli said quickly.

"No," Señor Rodriguez said again. "You go if you wish. You go with Dick."

"I don't know," Dick said, rubbing his chin and feigning doubt. "He's a fine young man, all right, but a mite more young than he is man. Of what use would a kid like him be to me?"

"I'm past fifteen," Poli responded. "I'll work for you if you wish. My father's given me leave and I've made my decision. Now you have to decide."

Dick slammed Poli on the back and grasped the boy's right hand in his own. "That's great news!" he said. "Why, there's no white man in all of Texas I'd rather have with me on the trail!"

"I'm not a white man," Poli said, and with his thumb he rubbed the scar on his wrist.

"I was going to offer you a dollar a day," Dick said. "Best I'll be able to do now, though, will be seven dollars a week. And that's my final offer. Now you decide."

The parade had left the town square. The crowd followed and Poli pushed past Dick, heading towards Military Plaza. Poli turned and spoke. "One week's pay in advance?" he asked.

"Sounds fair enough," Dick said. Then, reaching to his belt, he cried out: "Hey—who took my—?"

Poli handed Dick his leather money pouch. "Of what use would you be to me?" Poli asked and, seeing Dick's startled expression, he could not keep from smiling.

That night, as they sat out under a sky luminous with stars—a great dome that glittered as if sprayed with the finest Mexican silver—Señor Rodriguez told Poli that even before they talked with Dick, he'd known what he intended to do.

"I'll journey to Zaragosa," he said. "While you're away, I'll visit with your brothers and your sisters and see my grandchildren."

"And then?"

"Then I'll return to Texas."

"Yes."

"You were a gift to me, Policarpo—the son of my old years, and you've given me new life. That's why

I came north with you when your mother was gone and your brothers and sisters married. We have a better life here than we might ever have had in Mexico. I wanted to give you new life even as you had given it to me. I wanted to return the gift."

"Dick has to hire two more men and take in supplies," Poli said. "We leave in three days."

"Then I will leave in two," Señor Rodriguez said.

Chapter 11

POLI ON THE TRAIL

The surveying party moved north along the Old Spanish Trail, Dick and Poli riding a half-mile ahead of the others. There were ten men with them, each with a pack mule for transporting surveying instruments.

"I saw your father when he came through town yesterday," Dick said. "He told me he's going back to the place you were born in—to where the rest of your family is."

"But he'll return," Poli said. "Our home is here now, in Texas."

"I guess mine is too." Dick's tongue moved inside his cheek. "I love getting out on the trail like this, but it'd be good too if there was someplace to come back to at the end of the trip."

Abruptly, Dick turned his horse and rode back to the others.

Shortly after midday, the surveying party came upon a wooden sign:

THE CITY OF NEW BRAUNFELS

A Settlement From The Adelsverein

A quarter mile beyond, beside the Comal River, the German colonists were hard at work—cutting timber for their houses, clearing land for fall planting, digging wells, laying out streets. The treeless plain upon which they worked was amazingly similar to the land at Privilege Creek where Poli and his father had made their home.

To the south the plain was bounded by gently sloping hills, to the east by the Guadalupe River, and to the north and northwest by the crystal-clear waters of the Comal. Prince Solms-Braunfels rode around the settlement still attired in his fancy velvet and silk clothing, and while he supervised the work in progress two servants rode behind him.

"The water has a purity no mountain stream in the Alps can equal," the prince said to Dick and Poli when he joined them. "Yet the climate is like that of southern Italy. This is a truly wondrous land."

Five hundred more settlers would arrive before the end of the year, the prince said. Each person who signed on in Germany for the journey would be given passage, land, provisions, horses, tools, cattle, food, and a home.

"I see a new Germany here in America," the prince continued. "Since Prince Metternich will not allow us our national identity within the German Confederation, we will create our community here. And we will bring our poor with us. Under our guidance they too, with hard work, will earn their freedom."

All day long Dick and the prince studied maps; then they charted a provisional route, one that would link several new German settlements, the settlements to run in a westerly direction through the Hill Country.

The surveying party camped at New Braunfels for the night. In the morning the prince offered the men provisions for their journey. Due to the possibility of Indian attack, however, Poli suggested they travel lightly and take their food as they went along: fish from the Guadalupe, Cibolo, and Comal Rivers; deer, squirrel, wildcat, and turkey from the hills.

Each morning before the men broke camp Poli rode ahead as scout, his senses alert to any sign of hostile Indians. When he determined that there was no danger, he returned to the surveying party and worked along with them.

While they worked, the men left their horses in one place, taking only their mules with them; they made a strip map as they went along—staking out a probable road line with transits and chain. Poli carried the chain, which was sixty-six feet long and constructed of one hundred links. At intervals of three hundred yards the men made benchmarks—reference points to indicate

direction—and when they came to level country they used chain pins to mark these points. Where the mesquite grew high they drove metal-capped logs into the ground.

Dick taught Poli how to use the cross staff, which consisted of a long straight stick with two finely carved sighting grooves cut at right angles to one another, and how, after laying out triangles by sighting along these grooves, to calculate area. He taught him the fundamental rule of all surveying: that no matter what the form or the surface to be surveyed might be—square or rectangle, polygon or trapezoid—it could always be determined by subdividing it into triangles, and that to do this the fanciest instruments could not be more accurate than the chain and the cross staff.

Early on their eighth morning out of San Antonio, when Poli stopped by a creek to water Hermano he noticed that some of the grass was lower than the rest—a sign that horses had been there the day before. He walked along the bank, examining the marks in the earth. Then he mounted his horse and raced back to the surveying party.

"Kiowa," he said, as soon as he reached them.

"How many?" one of the men asked.

"Eight or ten, but they're on horseback and we're out in the open."

"With mules!"

"Where's Dick?" Poli asked.

"He went back to base camp with Jake and Tom."

"Come on, then," Poli said. "Leave the tools where they are and tie the mules to trees. They'll only slow us down."

The men worked swiftly. With Poli in the lead, they started back toward camp on foot. Before they travelled a quarter of a mile, however, they heard the sharp *crack!* of a rifle shot.

Poli rode ahead and the men ran behind him, their guns drawn. Poli listened carefully—there were more shots—and he knew at once that they had not all come from the three men left at the base camp.

"Fire your guns into the air!" Poli commanded. "The Kiowa have Dick and the others surrounded. Fire now!"

Poli urged Hermano on and soon saw the camp, where the Kiowa were circling two men. The men knelt back to back on the treeless plain, shooting and reloading as quickly as they could. Poli looked for the third man—Dick—but he was not there. Poli fired three shots. "Fire again!" he yelled to the men behind him. "Keep firing!" The men did as Poli told them to, and the Kiowa stopped, looking in the direction of the shots.

"Down!" Poli called, as soon as the surveyors reached him. "Everybody down. We don't want them to know how many of us there are."

Poli pointed to a thicket of pine trees on the south side of the plain. "Move to the woods there, but don't run. Get low to the ground and try to look like boulders."

"Like what?"

"If we all run at once, our moving bodies will tell

the Kiowa of our strength," Poli said. "One man at a
time. Crawl a short distance, squat, then wait until the
next man moves, and crawl again."

"What about Howard and the others?"

"Leave that to me," Poli said. "And keep firing."

Then Poli raced for the camp. When he was within
firing distance of the Kiowa he saw that there were five
of them: three shooting from horseback while two others
tried to round up the surveyors' horses. In the distance,
south toward the Comal, Poli spotted another group
of Kiowa. The leader of this group was darker than the
others—once a Negro slave, Poli guessed—and he wore
a tall stovepipe hat.

Poli reined Hermano in, unslung his carbine from
his shoulder, sighted, took a deep breath, held it, and
squeezed the trigger. The black Indian grabbed at his
shoulder, and fell to the ground. The Kiowa who were
shooting at Tom and Jake, and stealing the horses, now
sped off.

Poli rode to the two surveyors.

"They've got Howard surrounded," Jake yelled.
"Down there—by the horses!"

Poli raced on. In the ring of dust no more than
fifty yards ahead he saw a man on the ground.

A shot whistled by Poli's left ear. "Yi-yi-yi—!" he
yelled.

Dick was on one knee, the barrel of his pistol
balanced across his forearm.

"Yi-yi-yi—!" Poli cried again, and he let his body
fall from Hermano's back. The loop held him under the

armpit and a second later, galloping around the circle of Kiowa, his body shielded from them, his carbine in the crook of his arm, he fired at them from beneath Hermano's belly.

The Indians fled, joining the others at the spot where their wounded leader lay. The black Indian raised a lance in his good hand, urging his braves to stand and to fight. Poli let his own rifle drop to the ground, fixed his heel on Hermano's back and, reaching out with his right hand, his body still pressed to his horse's side, he charged toward Dick.

"Here I come," he called. "Get ready!!'

Dick took a last shot at the fleeing Indians, then shoved his pistol into his belt. Poli reached down and braced himself. He saw a bright patch of red on the ground where Dick was kneeling, and he saw that his friend rose in pain, clutching to a bleeding leg. He was upon him now, and Dick reached up and grabbed Poli's arm. Poli let himself drop lower, for leverage; then, his arm around Dick's waist, he pulled with all his strength.

Dick's boots bounded along the ground, but the two men held to one another. Dick grabbed at the braided rawhide in Hermano's mane.

"*Now!*" Poli cried, and he heaved upwards. His heel slipped slightly, but Dick's feet rose from the prairie and then he lay across Hermano's neck, above Poli.

Poli's heel slipped again; both feet touched the ground but, his shoulder still firmly held by the rawhide loop, he hoisted himself back so that he sat upright behind Dick.

"This way," Poli called to Jake and Tom. "The others are back there in the woods. Let's move out!"

Poli told them to gather as much gear as they could. He retrieved his rifle, then led the men and horses to the thicket of pine.

"We showed those devils," Jake said. "We sure drove the bastards off!"

"They only left to get others," Poli said. "We'll have to work quickly."

In the blackness of the forest, Poli knelt by Dick's side.

"You just leave me here and make a run for it," Dick said. "It's your only chance."

Poli put a wet cloth across Dick's forehead. "Rest now. We'll be all right."

Dick looked down at his leg, where Poli had cut out the bullet and wrapped the wound. "Listen," Dick said. "I'm in charge and I'm ordering you to get out of here. Just leave me a few guns and some ammunition. That's an order!"

"I'm not in the Army," Poli replied.

"I'm not either." Weakened by the loss of blood, Dick spoke softly. "Listen, Poli, if anything happens, you'll find a piece of paper in my wallet. It has a name and address on it: General Lucius Howard, in Smithtown, Virginia. And when you write to him, you—"

"Shh," Poli said. "You rest now. We'll need you later."

Poli told the men to build up the fire and to find

other clearings in the woods, to start new fires. "When you've done that," he said, "find all the scraps of cloth you can—tear your extra clothing into small pieces, and gather up strips of rawhide, and when—"

"Are you crazy?" one of the men said. It was John Carter, a surly man who had resented Poli's presence from the journey's outset. "There's only a dozen of us. Build up the fires for what? You might as well put a map and a welcome sign out on the trail so them red devils can find their way to our graves more easy."

"The Indians won't attack if they think there are many of us," Poli stated. "We'll build fires and then we'll talk and shout and call to one another. Some of us will bark like dogs. We'll provoke the horses and mules, and when . . . "

"You men can follow this dumb Mex to the happy hunting grounds if you want," Carter said, "but I'm getting out now. Anyone who wants to can come with me. If the kid had done his job right, none of this would've happened in the first place."

"The Indians won't attack if they don't know our numbers," Poli repeated. "A Kiowa fears being killed at night because he believes that if he dies in darkness his spirit will wander forever in darkness."

"And in the morning?"

"We'll be gone," Poli replied. "On the trail back to San Antonio."

When the sun had set and Poli heard the Kiowa war cries come to them across the prairie, the surveyors were sitting by five separate campfires, cutting up cloth-ing and stitching the pieces together.

They talked and they sang and they shouted; they barked and they hollered and they banged on pots and pans. Poli yelled out commands in Spanish and in Comanche, and Dick called out orders in German. The men poked their mules and horses with sticks, the animals whinnied and brayed . . . and the Kiowa did not enter the forest.

When Poli was certain the Kiowa raiding party had retreated for the night, he showed the men how to tie the cloth pads to the hooves of the horses and mules so that the animals would travel noiselessly. Then he rigged a *travois* to Dick's horse—two lodgepoles har-nessed to the horse's flanks, buffalo skins stretched between the poles—and Dick lay upon it. The men hung pots and pans from the trees, built up the fires and, Poli in the lead, they moved silently from the woods.

Poli led the men back toward San Antonio on a southeasterly route. By following the flights of birds, he located streams and water holes. On the fourth morn-ing of their return journey, while the men and horses rested beside a narrow brook on logs of bleached cot-tonwood, Poli spotted a cave in the rocks above them.

He climbed to the cave and, taking with him some oily patches of cloth which he spiked on a branch, he made his way down through a damp, winding tunnel until the light from the outside world was gone. Then he lit the oily patches and saw that he was inside an enormous underground chamber where fantastic shapes rose from the ground and hung from above. He felt he had entered a dream that would never end.

He slipped his knife from its sheath and moved cautiously forward. A formation of rocks in the center of the chamber looked like a castle Poli had seen in picture books—the kind he imagined Prince Solms-Braunfels once lived in. He imagined the prince and his followers passing from the castle across a drawbridge and onto a road that led down to the sea.

He saw daggers, owls, loaves of bread. Against a far wall, he saw a giant cougar, crouching below a waterfall. Then something cold and wet hit him on the back of his neck. He looked up—drops of water were poised at the ends of long spears.

Poli heard a roaring noise. He looked around, saw openings on all sides of the chamber, but could not recognize the one by which he had entered. He felt lost and frightened suddenly—like a little boy. This was the way he had felt when his father had left him alone, years before, at Privilege Creek.

The dark recesses of the chamber were like the deep night sky, and that sky became a forest without end and without familiar trails. As men feared death, Poli recalled his father saying, so children feared to go into the dark.

Poli turned. He looked first at one opening, then at another, then at the curious, misshapen rocks that lay across the cave's floor. All paths might lead to danger, he knew. There was no safe exit, no way of *not* being lost. The roaring drew near, rumbling and slamming against the chamber's walls. Poli ran to his left, held his torch inside a tunnel, but could not see to the tunnel's end. He looked back and saw a monstrous lizard gazing hungrily at him, its jaws open . . .

Poli closed his eyes. He was not a little boy, afraid his father would never return. Nor was he a boy safe in bed, in Zaragosa, his mother by his side, assuring him that his nightmares would go away. Poli opened his eyes, surveyed the cave floor steadily until he saw the impress of his own footprints in the damp red dust. He followed the prints, found the opening through which he had first come. A few seconds later he emerged into sunlight and stood on the rock, seeing the surveyors below.

He scurried down and sat beside Dick, telling him about what he had seen.

"Those rocks are called stalactites and stalagmites," Dick said. "Not far from West Point there's a cave like the one you've just seen. Howe Cavern, it's called. When I studied geology we went there, learned all about it."

"But who made them?" Poli asked. "How could such castles and palaces just happen?"

"Water," Dick said, smiling. "Just plain old water. Dripping down in darkness, day after day, year after year, century after century."

John Carter stood above them, at the entrance to the cave.

"Don't go in there," Poli said.

"Why not? You seemed to like it well enough to

stay a while." Carter laughed. "Listen, boy, I heard you talkin' to Dick about them castles and treasure been in this cave for centuries. You don't think I'm gonna let you take it all for yourself, do you?"

"Don't go in there," Poli said again.

"This kid's just like them Injuns he grew up with," Carter said to the others. "You can't trust a one of 'em. After we get back to San Antonio, him and Howard'll come back and divvy up all the loot, be rich forever."

Carter entered the cave.

"Don't mind what he says," Dick said, his arm around Poli's shoulder.

"I don't," Poli said.

"Carter's a mean-spirited son of a bitch. Not worth your time. I'm glad you didn't go after him."

"Me too," Poli said, and he smiled.

A few seconds later Carter burst from the cave. "Get back—get back everybody!" he screamed. "The devil's in there! The devil's after me! Help! Help . . . !"

A moment passed. Then a fat black bear lumbered out of the cave, spotted Carter, and pursued him. Carter fled down a slope, straight into the brook, screaming that the devil was after him.

The bear stopped at the water's edge, rose to his full height of nearly seven feet, roared mightily, then dropped to all fours and crawled sleepily back to its cave.

Chapter 12

SEÑOR RODRIGUEZ

There's Comanche now, too. Penateka," Jack Hays said. He looked hard at Poli. "Several bands have taken to raiding farms on the outskirts of town."

"As soon as my leg's healed," Dick said, "I want to get out again, finish mapping that road."

"Right," Hays said. "But this time you'll be protected, Dick. I'm sending cavalry with you and giving you a commission in the Rangers. Figure that way, you can be in charge—you know the region better'n anyone—and the men can take their orders direct from you."

"But I . . . "

"No buts," Hays said. "We must convince settlers we can make this region safe for 'em, and by God we're gonna do it. You'll be Lieutenant Richard Howard and there'll be no questions asked, hear?"

"Maybe," Dick said. "If Poli gets a commission too."

Hays hesitated. "He's only a Mexican kid," Hays

said. "And you know my men won't like the idea of . . ."

"And there'll be no questions asked, hear?" Dick said. "Because if you want me, you have to take Poli too."

A half-hour later, two beaming officers of the Texas Rangers emerged from Captain Jack Hays's headquarters: Lieutenant Richard Howard and Corporal José Policarpo Rodriguez.

For a week Poli helped Dick lay in supplies; at night he rode to his home at Privilege Creek and slept there. On September 12, 1844, when the surveying party left San Antonio, Señor Rodriguez had still not returned from Mexico.

Poli saw signs of small Indian bands—Kiowa, Comanche, and Arapaho—but due, he figured, to the presence of the sixteen Texas Rangers, the Indians did not harass the surveying party.

In the areas where the towns of Castell, Leiningen, and Meerholz would one day lie, the surveyors made camp and, along with three German colonists, laid out new settlements. The party then followed the North Llano River as far west as the Angelo Draw.

Late one afternoon four and a half weeks later, the men returned to the town of New Braunfels; Poli collected his pay, said goodby to Dick and, without lingering, rode straight for Privilege Creek.

To his delight, a campfire was burning in front of his home, and in the house itself a lantern shone. Poli was eager to see his father—to hear about his family and friends, to tell his father of all that he had seen, but when he reined Hermano in beside the campfire and dismounted, it was Eagle Blood and not his father who came out of the house.

"His spirit has been waiting for your return," Eagle Blood said, and he embraced his brother.

Señor Rodriguez lay under the white buffalo skin, his eyes glazed, his body still. Poli took his father's hand in his own. Señor Rodriguez smiled. "I knew you'd come," he said.

"Save your strength," Poli said. "Don't talk—"

"No," Señor Rodriguez said. "Now that you're home, I have the strength I need."

They had been apart for less than two months, yet his father seemed to be twenty years older. Poli looked into his father's brown eyes and saw there the man he knew when he was a boy in Zaragosa. The eyes shone like stones that had been polished for centuries by moving streams. Poli recalled his father giving him chocolate, telling him that the Aztecs had used the cacao beans, from which chocolate was made, for money.

Poli touched his own stomach. *Then this is my bank!* he had said, and his father had laughed with happiness.

"Now that you're here, my spirit can take its leave." Señor Rodriguez shivered. "Once more I've seen my sons and daughters and my grandchildren, my brothers and sisters and friends. I'm glad we came to Texas."

Señor Rodriguez tried to sit up. Poli put a hand behind his father's head, helped him.

"The life in Mexico is still hard for them. I've told

them about our home, and perhaps some of them will now come and join you here." Señor Rodriguez pointed to a wooden chest. "Among my belongings you'll find a piece of paper, Poli. Later—don't leave me now—you'll see that the paper is the deed to our land, my gift to you . . . "

Señor Rodriguez lay back down. He coughed. Poli took a water bag from the floor and set the opening gently to his father's mouth.

A few minutes later, Poli emerged from the house. He looked at Eagle Blood and said nothing. He walked away, down to the Medina. In the darkness, he heard the water rushing downstream as if it would tumble southwards forever.

He looked into the sky, found the North Star. When he was a boy, his father told him the story of the great New Fire ceremony of the Aztecs. The Aztecs performed this rite once every fifty-two years. They let all their fires die, extinguished the old altar fire in their temple, and destroyed their household possessions. Then for five days they waited—fasting, praying, tearing at their hair. For five days and nights, children were marched back and forth in their houses, since sleep on the fated evening of the New Fire would turn them into rats.

At sunset on the fifth day the priests and the people ascended Huixachtecatl, the Hill of the Star, and waited at the summit, scanning the sky until a group of stars—the Pleiades—reached the center of the heavens: the sign that the world would continue.

The priests then kindled a new fire and sent runners with torches lit from that fire to light the altars and temples of every village and town, and from the altars and temples the people bore the flames to their hearths. When dawn came on the sixth day, the people of Mexico feasted, then set to work again—restoring their temples, making new furniture and tools, preparing the land for crops.

"Since your father died a brave and happy man," Eagle Blood said, "we believe he'll be brave and happy forever in the spirit world."

Poli had stayed awake all night, gazing at the heavens, recalling the sound of his father's voice, the touch of his father's hands and lips. Now he stood outside the house with Eagle Blood.

"What will you do now?" Eagle Blood asked.

"What will you do now?" Poli replied.

"There's a great war coming, and it won't be between our tribes, or between Indians and white men, or Texans and Mexicans."

Poli nodded. He had listened to Dick Howard and the men talk about it during the trip—how Texas might become part of the United States of America. He told Eagle Blood what he knew.

"Sam Houston is no longer your president," Eagle Blood said. "He knew the ways of Indians and we never feared to talk with him."

"But the others?"

Eagle Blood scooped up a handful of dirt and flung

some to his right and some to his left, meaning, Poli
knew, that the words of others went both one way and
the other and not, like the truth, straight ahead.

"My father's been gone for four years, and each
year our hunting grounds are smaller and the buffalo,
like the numbers of our tribe, fewer," Eagle Blood said.
"If Texas becomes part of the Union and defeats Mexico, our lands will be taken from us, as the lands of
other tribes have been taken. They'll set us to live upon
their reservations."

Poli touched the scar on his wrist. He waited.

"And if Mexico should defeat Texas and take the
land, they'll use us as they always have. They'll take
vengeance upon all Comanches for the evil some
Comanches have done. How can I be my father's son?"

"I'll bury my father here, on our land," Poli stated.

"*Your* land?" Eagle Blood said. He stood and spoke
as if he were addressing his tribe. "If the Texans had
kept out of our country, there might have been peace!
But you Texans have taken from us the earth where the
grass grew thickest and the timber was best. The white
man now possesses the country which we loved, and
we wish only to wander on the prairie until we die."

"We were boys here together," Poli said. "We are
brothers forever. Whatever I possess—"

"Now your people want to put us on reservations,
to make medicine lodges for us to dwell in." Eagle Blood
slashed the air with his hand, as if slaughtering an
animal. His voice was strong and harsh, like Chief Tosh-
a-wah's. "But I was born upon the prairie, where the

wind blew free and there was nothing to break the light of the sun. I was born where there were no fences and everything drew a free breath. I want to die there, not within walls. Do not ask me to give up the buffalo for the sheep!"

Eagle Blood turned away in fury and mounted his horse.

Poli grabbed his brother's hand and held fast. "I am a Texan now and I don't ask you to give up anything."

"But you help those who do!" Eagle Blood's eyes blazed with anger. "You're still your father's *niño.*" Eagle Blood tore his hand from Poli's grasp. "It is time for the snake to strike—for the eagle is moving westward with speed and with force. Be careful. A white man may be old and foolish, but a Comanche may not. A foolish Comanche dies young. Be careful, my brother."

"*Vaya con dios,*" Poli said.

Eagle Blood gazed downwards at Poli and, momentarily, his gaze softened. "May our fathers forever dwell in peace," he said, and then he rode south.

Chapter 13

THE BIG BEND

Poli examined the broken twigs and stones. Their patterns told him what he did not wish to know.

"Comanche?" Dick asked.

"Yes," Poli said.

"They must have passed this way at least a week ago, though," Dick said. "I don't see signs of campfires."

"When their numbers are few the Comanches make no fires." Poli kicked dirt onto the twigs and stones. "These Comanches are searching for food and horses." He looked at Dick. "And revenge."

Nearly a year had passed since Señor Rodriguez's death, and during that year the Texas Congress had voted in favor of annexation by the United States of America; that same month, General Woll formally declared war, maintaining that Texas was still part of Mexico.

Woll's army did not cross the Rio Grande. Instead,

it waited to see whether or not the government of the United States would annex Texas and permit it to join the Union as a slave-holding state. The United States considered the eastern boundary of the Republic of Texas to be the Permanent Indian Frontier. By virtue of the Indian Removal Act, it was forcing almost all American Indians from their lands, sending them west to reservations and to the hunting grounds of the Kiowa and Comanche. Whenever Poli found evidence of Indian bands, as he did now, he led his surveying parties away from them.

This time Poli and Dick were farther from home than usual—in the southwest region of Texas, undertaking a topographic survey for the Republic of Texas. There were forty-five men in their group—sixteen surveyors, three engineers, and two dozen Texas Rangers under the command of Captain Jim Brace. Poli was the guide, Dick the chief surveyor.

Poli led the men along the Rio Grande for several miles and then, where the Comanche trail turned south towards Mexico, he turned his party north, along the border of the Chisos Mountains.

"But that's solid limestone ahead," Dick said.

"There's a pass," Poli replied. "Once we're through the pass, we'll be in a valley that cuts through the stone. Indians would never let themselves be closed in by the walls. We'll be safe. There's only one problem."

"What's that?" Dick asked.

"I know there's a way in," Poli said. "But I don't know if there's a way out."

The men followed Poli through the narrow pass and into a valley that seemed to stretch ahead of them forever. To either side the limestone table formations extended in long horizontal layers and Poli understood, from what Dick taught him, that the history of the earth could be read in these formations.

Soon the valley widened and the straight bluffs along either side became jagged, reminding Poli of the shapes he had seen in the underground cave—except that these were enlarged a thousandfold. Then the jagged peaks gave way to high hills that were crowned with dark masses of red-black basalt.

Poli suggested the men camp beside a small stream tucked into a triangular indentation in the hills. That night, the Rangers stood guard and made no fires.

In the morning they set out again and within an hour the valley disappeared. The mountains to either side suddenly vanished, as if severed by an enormous sword, and Poli found himself leading the men through a forest of dead trees.

He dismounted, examined the trees and, to his surprise, found that they were hard as stone.

"A petrified forest," Dick said. He explained that these ghostly trees were actually fossils—that the forest itself, like the valley through which they had just passed, had once been covered over with water. Through many thousands of centuries, and without losing their shapes, the wood of the trees had been replaced, cell by cell, with minerals.

The men rode on. The petrified forest ended and

the horses now trampled not over tree trunks but across yellowed grass. Then they passed through another petrified forest and when this forest ended, mountains reappeared as if they were apparitions. Below these mountains enormous canyons dropped down steeply from the earth's surface.

Dick and the engineers sounded the canyons and determined that some of them were nearly two thousand feet deep. With compasses and chain, the men mapped the land.

On their third day through the region that would one day be known as the Big Bend Country, Poli led the men from the canyons to land that was semi-arid, yet covered with lush green vegetation and brilliant wild-flowers: poppy, Indian paintbrush, phlox, purple sage, wild roses—with juniper, verbena, and cactus blossoms. The colors were more dazzling and beautiful than any Poli had ever seen.

Poli shook his head—it was as if the bright colors were roaring through his head—and then he heard Dick's voice, shouting at him.

"Are you all right?" Dick asked.

The roaring came on again, like that of waves crashing to shore, and Poli hardly heard Dick.

"Sounds like a blizzard," one of the surveyors said. "But the sky's clear."

Poli put his ear to the wind, listened, and then he laughed.

"I taste honey!" he shouted, and he raced ahead,

straight into the roaring.

When he came to the edge of a bluff, he pointed below, to a boulder. "There's the notch—where Indians have been letting down their men by rope for years. Get me some oily rags."

Dick put his arm around Poli and shouted into Poli's ear: "And that's Maravillas Creek below—we're still a long ways from home, but the valley did have a way out."

Poli rolled the rags into a bundle and tied the end to a stick. He hitched one end of a rope to his waist, the other to the saddle on Dick's horse. Dick mounted his horse and as the men let Poli down the side of the bluff, Dick slowly backed away until the line was taut. Poli clambered down the side of the cliff. Some fifty feet above the creek, he found the hole, set fire to the rags, and stuck the flaming torch in.

Then he yelled and the men hauled him up. A line of smoke rose up the side of the bluff after him, and the bees came roaring behind it.

"Aieee—!" one of the surveyors cried, and ran.

"Those things'll eat us alive!" cried another, and he took off after the first man.

Poli laughed. "The smoke and wind will drive the bees towards the water," he said.

An hour later the men lowered Poli again. He unsheathed his knife, reached in, and began to cut away at the honeycomb.

The men stored most of the honey in deerskin bags for the return journey, but that night they celebrated, enjoying their favorite meal: a side of venison roasted on a ramrod, basted with bear oil, and dipped in honey.

They sang and they drank and they ate. When they were through carousing, however, and were bedding down for the night, they discovered that nearly half their horses were gone. The two Texas Rangers who had been standing guard were dead, arrows in their chests.

Chapter 14

JOURNEY HOME

There are only nine or ten of them," Poli told Dick after he examined the marks on the trail. "Their own horses are weak, the Indians themselves probably close to starvation. They'll be back."

"But without enough horses for our men, how can *we* get back?" Dick asked.

"We can't stay here," Poli said. "They know we won't attack and they know we can't move fast. What they'll try to do is more of the same—pick us off one or two at a time."

Dick nodded. "What if the surveyors double up and ride the mules? We could leave the gear here . . . "

" . . . and the Rangers could flank us on either side," Poli said. "Good. As long as our strength is at least equal to theirs, they'll be scared of attacking us."

A man screamed. Poli whirled around. From a high rock where he was standing lookout, a Texas Ranger tumbled forward, clutching at an arrow, trying to pull it from his stomach. He bounced down the incline of rocks, then lay still. A snake moved from its shelter in the rocks, passed across the man's broken skull.

Poli mounted Hermano, circled the camp quickly, spotted the Indians, then raced back to Dick, and to Jim Brace.

"They've made our decision for us," Poli said. He pointed to a stone wall near where the Ranger had been hit. "If we can all get to the stone wall under that ridge, they won't be able to surround us. We'll make our stand there."

Brace called out commands to his men, and Dick told the surveyors and engineers to follow the Rangers.

The wall Poli pointed to was some fifty yards away and the Rangers doubled up on their horses, the surveyors running behind them, Dick and Poli guarding the rear.

The men made it to the wall before the Comanches came in sight, then tied their horses together and formed a semicircle in front of the horses, the Rangers on one knee, their rifles cocked, bullets between their teeth for reloading.

The Comanches reined their horses in; to Poli's surprise there were more than thirty of them, which explained why they were not afraid to attack. The Comanches who had killed the two Rangers the night before were only a small part of the band then, sent to gather horses for the others.

Poli spoke quickly to Dick and to Jim Brace, and they passed the word along: The men were to hold their fire until Poli gave the word; then each man was to pick out a single Indian and shoot to kill.

The Comanche chief rode a magnificent brown mustang, its black tail ornamented with silver and gold ribbons. The chief's chest was bare and in the early morning sun his body glistened as if oiled. His braided hair hung past his shoulders, and his face and chest were radiant with crimson war paint.

"The chief is mine," Poli said. "If I can get him, the others will lose heart."

"And if you don't?" Dick asked.

The chief's horse reared up, then charged forward, and his braves followed, shouting and shrieking. Poli bent to one knee and sighted the chief along his gun barrel.

The chief galloped directly for the center of the semicircle. Poli held his breath, to keep his gun steady. But then the mustang shifted, swerving to the left. Poli slung his gun sideways and saw that the chief, by his maneuver, was now thundering down upon their position from the right, no more than fifty feet away, his lance poised in the air.

"*Now!*" Poli cried, and he squeezed the trigger. The chief continued to plunge forward, even as the Rangers and surveyors began firing. Several Comanches fell from their horses, but the others pressed on. Poli had no time to reload. He drew his bowie knife and stood.

The Comanche chief was almost upon him and Poli saw that the red which streamed across his chest was not only war paint; Poli's shot had been true.

Poli looked into the warrior's face and saw that the eyes were younger than he had expected, and that they were fixed upon his own face, not with the narrow anguish of his pain, but with astonishment.

The lance fell from the chief's hand. Poli stepped forward. The other Comanches were less than twenty yards behind their chief. His eyes still fixed upon Poli's face, the chief's neck suddenly snapped backwards in agony, as if only at that moment had the bullet entered his chest. He cried out and fell from his horse.

Seeing their leader fall, the Comanches reined their horses in. "Forward!" Jim Brace yelled, and the Rangers moved from their kneeling position, raced ten feet, kneeled again, fired.

The Comanches retreated.

"Hold your fire!" Poli called.

"Don't know how you waited so damned long," Jim Brace said to Poli. "I guess everything I heard about you's true."

"Got that painted devil good," one of the surveyors shouted. "Never seen a look like the one on that bastard's face when he knew he was done for!"

Poli glared at the man, but said nothing.

He walked toward the dead Comanche, and lifted him in his arms. He turned.

"I'm going to take this Comanche to his brothers, and if any man tries to stop me I'll kill him."

Then Poli walked across the prairie toward the

Comanche band. When he was some twenty yards away, he called out in their own dialect, "I am Poli, brother of Eagle Blood!"

Poli set the body on the ground. Two warriors rode forward and dismounted. Poli recognized them as braves with whom he had once played Comanche games by the Medina.

"You've given us our leader," one of them said. "We give you your horses."

"Gather your slain and your wounded," Poli said. "He was his father's son, the child of Tosh-a-wah. He was my brother. Like yours, my heart too is broken, and in my mouth there is a taste that is bitter, like that of gourds."

Poli walked back across the prairie. He told Dick and Jim to have their men put away their guns.

Then Poli picked up his rifle. The barrel was still warm. He walked to the wall which had defended the men from the rear, raised the rifle above his head, and brought it crashing down upon stone.

The surveying party reached San Antonio early on the evening of January 5, 1846. To their surprise, the town still seemed to be celebrating the New Year. Brightly-colored lights adorned the main street, bands were playing, Texans and Mexicans were dancing in the street . . .

For word had just been received, Poli and Dick learned, that the Republic of Texas had been annexed by the United States of America, and would become the twenty-eighth state in the Union.

The Rangers and surveyors whooped and hollered, shot their pistols into the air and joined in the festivities. Dick and Poli rode out of town.

They soon reached Fort San Antonio. The Lone Star no longer flew above the fort; instead the Stars and Stripes of the United States of America fluttered in the evening breeze.

Poli and Dick entered the stockade, told the orderly that they were there to report to Captain Hays. Then they stood on the porch of the officers' quarters, looking out at the parade grounds where several peacock and deer moved about peacefully as they often did.

"You've never asked me, all the times we've been together, but it's time you knew something," Dick said. "General Lucius Howard—the name I gave you—is my father. I was supposed to be General Howard also, except that I wasn't ever real good at taking orders." Dick spoke slowly. "And I never really wanted to live the life he lived. I like the life I've make here, where I'm free to travel and work when I want and where I want."

A deer approached, then shied away.

"I went to the Point—to please him, mostly—did well enough for three years. Then something snapped inside me—just buckled and gave way. The details don't matter—mostly I was just tired of living by the rules other people set, so I got restless and bored and rebellious. I drank and I gambled and I fought—you must have guessed—and they expelled me."

"If war comes, what will you do?"

"Texas is my home now," Dick said. "I've had a good life here. I'll fight for Texas." He paused. "Not for the United States—but for Texas. Do you understand?"

The door to Jack Hays's office opened. The orderly told them that Hays was ready to see them.

"And you?" Dick asked.

"Texas is my home too," Poli said, and to his surprise he found that the confusion—the divided heart—that had been within him for so long, was gone.

In his mind he imagined a young Mexican boy riding off through tunnels, and the tunnels, he knew, were in his own mind and they led to a dark and beautiful cave. He could live in that cave, he sensed, and he could bring the light of the world into it.

"My father is buried here and my friends live here. But I'll always be a Mexican. I was born there, and my family still live there. Who can I fight against? No matter which side I choose I'd have to kill friends and brothers. And like the Comanche, no matter who I fight—Mexican or Texan—I'd be doomed."

"Then you won't fight, will you?" Dick said.

"I won't fight," Poli said.

Postscript

In 1846, war broke out between Mexico and the United States, and Poli remained true to his word. He stayed on his land at Privilege Creek and enlisted in the San Antonio Home Guard, defending citizens of the area from bands of marauding outlaws and Indians.

When the Mexican-American war ended in 1848, Poli went out on the trail again, with Dick Howard and the United States Army. For nearly a decade he worked as a guide, exploring new territory and establishing new roads, leading settlers and soldiers across the Texas he knew and loved.

Then, in 1856, camels were brought to America, and Poli was given a new job: he became the first official Keeper of the Camels for the U. S. Army, living at Camp Verde—a few miles from his home at Privilege Creek—and working with the Arab camel drivers.

When the Civil War erupted between the states in 1861 and Texas chose to fight with the Confederacy, Poli again chose not to fight. He loved Texas—but he had also worked with the Army of the United States for a dozen years; many of his friends from that Army would now be fighting, and dying, for the Union.

Once again Poli returned to his home at Privilege Creek, and once again he helped to defend the San Antonio region from raiders and outlaws; the people of San Antonio elected him Captain of the Home Guard, and he served in this position until peace came in 1865.

The experiments with the camels died with the war. Although some camels remained at Camp Verde, and although they proved themselves more suited to the terrain and weather of the southwest than mules, the U. S. Congress refused to vote any more funds for the experiment. Camels had been Jefferson Davis's idea when he was Secretary of War in President Pierce's cabinet. Since Davis had been President of the Confederacy, all things connected with him were now scorned by U. S. Congressmen. The camels were sold in March of 1866, and when they left Camp Verde, Poli left the Army.

He returned to his home at Privilege Creek, but this time he did not return alone. He had married and soon, in the house he and his father had built, he was raising his own sons and daughters.

In 1872, he became a guide again—a guide for the souls of his people. Poli spent the remainder of his life as a Methodist minister and missionary to Mexicans in Texas.

When he died, on March 22, 1914, the trails he had blazed were already well-traveled roads and highways, and the places he had discovered, such as Cascade Caverns and the Big Bend Country, were known far beyond Texas. Railroads did the work mules had done, and that camels might have done. The Comanches lived on reservations.

The State of Texas, a Republic whose population numbered in the thousands when Poli had first crossed the Rio Grande, had over four million people.

José Policarpo Rodriguez was buried next to a stone church near the Medina, a church he built himself—a church set in front of a rugged mountain known to the people of the region as Poli's Peak. In his last years Poli often sat in front of the church, watching his children and grandchildren, and remembering what the land had been like when he and Eagle Blood had been boys together.

Poli Comes to Texas: a Reader's Guide

Questions for Discussion

1. In 1839, when he is 10 years old, Poli leaves his home in Zaragosa, Mexico, and, with his father, travels north to the Republic of Texas. They settle in the San Antonio area, where they have neither friends nor family, and are, truly, strangers in a strange land.

- *Have you ever been uprooted from a place you love—or can you imagine being uprooted and having to settle in a new place, and make a new life? Tell us what it was like, or what you imagine it would be like.*

2. The friendship between Poli and a young Comanche, Eagle Blood, is at the heart of *Poli: A Mexican Boy in Early Texas.* Soon after Poli and his father settle in the Hill Country near San Antonio, Poli is taken in by Eagle Blood's tribe, the Penatekas, and educated in their ways. He learns their customs, their history, and the meanings of their personal ornaments and grooming, whether for war or for peace. And he learns to ride horses in the amazing ways the Comanches rode horses. On the very day they meet, we read: "The two boys streaked across the prairie, side by side, the warm morning wind in their faces. A friend, Poli told himself. A friend of my own!"

- *Why is Eagle Blood's friendship so important to Poli?*
- *What might his life have been like if, when he first came to Tex-*

as, he had not met Eagle Blood and discovered the ways of the Comanches?

• *Do you have, or have ever had, a best friend who felt like a brother or sister?*

3. "If the Texans had kept out of my country," Eagle Blood's father, Chief Tosh-a-wah, intones, "there might have been peace. Oh do not ask us to give up the buffalo for the sheep! Do not ask us to give up the buffalo for the sheep!"

• *What does Chief Tosh-a-wah mean by these words?*

• *Can you understand the passion with which he and Eagle Blood, through the years, repeat this chant again and again?*

4. "Texas is going to be good to us," Poli's father tells him on the evening before they break camp and move into the city of San Antonio.

• *Do his words come true?*

• *Has the state you live in been good to you and your family? If so, in what ways?*

5. Poli lives through both the Mexican-American War and the Civil War, yet chooses to fight in neither of them. Instead, he becomes Captain of the San Antonio Home Guard.

• *What are the conflicts that bring about Poli's conflicting loyalties—his divided heart—and what do you think of the choices he makes?*

•*What would you have done in Poli's situation?*

6. Poli lived through the most formative years of Texas history—when it changed from being part of Mexico, to becoming a separate Republic, and, finally, to becoming the 28th state of the United States of America. During his long life he was many things—a guide, a surveyor, a hunter, a ranchman, a gunsmith, an Indian fighter, a Keeper of Camels for the U. S. Army, a Texas Ranger, an explorer, and a preacher.

- *Which parts of Poli's life interest you most?*

- *Do you think it's still possible for a young man or woman to have a life as rich and adventurous as Poli had?*

- *What parts of your life, so far, have been unexpected and/or adventurous?*

- *What adventures do you hope to have? Tell us about them.*

About the author and illustrator

Jay Neugeboren is the author of 21 books, including three prize-winning novels (*The Stolen Jew, Before My Life Began, The American Sun & Wind Moving Picture Company*), two books of award-winning non-fiction (*Imagining Robert, Transforming Madness*), and four collections of prize-winning stories. His stories and essays have appeared widely, in *The New York Review of Books, The New York Times, The American Scholar, Ploughshares, Black Clock*, etc., and in dozens of anthologies, including *Best American Short Stories, O. Henry Prize Stories*, and *Penguin Modern Stories*. He lives in New York City.

Tom Leamon has illustrated many books for young people, including Robert McClung's *Grizzly Adams*.